REBEL GIRL

by

ROXANE BEAUFORT

GW00370394

Chimera (ki-mir'ə, kī-)
a creation of the imagination,
a wild fancy...

CHIMERA
books.co.uk

Rebel Girl first published in 2010 by
Chimera Books Ltd
PO Box 152
Waterlooville
Hants
PO8 9FS
United Kingdom

Printed and bound in the UK by
Cox & Wyman, Reading.

ISBN 978-1-903931-89-9

This novel is fiction – in real life practice safe sex

REBEL GIRL

Roxane Beaufort

Chimera *(kī-mîr'ə, kĭ-)* a creation of the
imagination, a wild fantasy

Judith stood in the centre of the cell, looking around her. The only light was from a window high up in the stone wall, and this was protected by iron bars. There was no bed, no chair, nothing, and if Steven intended to force himself on her, then it would have to be against the wall or on the bare brick floor. Did he want to starve her into submission, seeing her grovel? His behaviour suggested he would. She had hurt his pride, and this was all important to him.

Prelude

England 1643

The woman lying on the bed stretched voluptuously, rejoicing in the freedom from clothing. Though a leader of fashion, she was happiest when nude.

She ran her hands over her smooth white skin, luxuriating in the feel of softness and warmth, admiring the sheer physical perfection of her body. She walked her fingers down her belly and played with the foxy curls at her bush, tugging at them gently, each springy hair sending messages to her clitoris. She could feel herself moistening.

The room was magnificent, candles in branching silver holders flickering over tapestries, oak panelling, gilt, ornately scrolled plaster-work, and the dimly seen paintings of gods and goddesses cavorting across the ceiling. This was one of the finest houses Oxford could provide, befitting her position as Isobel, Baroness Thorley, and she had rented it from a nobleman who had retired abroad at the start of the conflict between King Charles I and his Parliament.

A log crackled, collapsing in a shower of sparks, flames shooting up the wide chimney, casting highlights over the face of the young soldier who stood watching her, an elbow resting on the mantelpiece. It scintillated on the swept-hilt sword hanging by its baldric over the back of a chair. It flashed over gold braid trimming blue velvet, lace-edged ruffles, and breeches ending in supple leather boots. So handsome a warrior. Isobel's nipples tingled in anticipation.

She sat up, stuffing a pillow behind her back, her full breasts barely hidden by the russet curls tumbling across them. Reaching for the decanter on the bedside table, she poured measures of brandy into two goblets.

'Will you drink with me, captain?' she said, her voice low and husky.

The soldier smiled, dark eyes glittering. 'Of course, baroness,' she replied, and loosened the ties of her doublet, then ran a finger under her neckband, freeing that, too.

Isobel continued confidently, 'I'm so happy to see you again, Antonia. There's been so much talk of your exploits, your courage on the battlefield, and your closeness to Prince Rupert.'

Antonia came nearer, moving with feline grace. She had removed her jacket, and the full-sleeved lawn shirt lay open to the waist, her olive skin contrasting with its whiteness. She paused by the bed and took the glass Isobel offered.

'To His Majesty,' she said, and raised it to her lips.

'His Majesty,' Isobel repeated, and ran her tongue provocatively round the rim before taking a sip.

Sounds filtered up from the street, shouts and bursts of laughter and singing. 'The troops are enjoying leave,' she observed.

'Oxford has become one huge brothel,' Antonia answered sombrely. 'A gaming house, a tavern, a place where one can forget the slaughter, the bloodshed, the sheer idiocy of it all. What are we doing – fighting our own people? Civil war is the most terrible of all.'

'They rebelled against the king. It had to be stopped,' Isobel reminded. For her part war had presented a glorious opportunity for adventure, travel and excitement, providing a plethora of lovers. She didn't regret it one bit. Especially on occasions like tonight.

She could smell the girl soldier, that intoxicating combination of leather, the personal odour of her hair and the musky aroma of her body. With a bold gesture Isobel opened the shirt wider and feasted her eyes on the bare flesh. She hungered to taste her, to lick the salty sweat that sheened the hollow of her throat, to lap at the tight, hard nipples, and go lower, dipping her tongue into the navel and lower still to savour the stronger flavour trapped in the hair covering her mound. It was black, she well knew, matching the mane that fell in ringlets across Antonia's shoulders and halfway down her back.

She patted the side of the bed. 'Sit and tell what you've been up to,' she said, and her fingers fastened on the shirt sleeve, feeling the hardness and steely strength of the muscles beneath.

'Do we have to play these games? We both know why I'm here and it isn't to talk about military campaigns,' Antonia said ironically, and reached out for her.

'Wait,' Isobel commanded. 'You know I like to hear about the fighting. It excites me. Describe what you do to your women prisoners. Are you harsh? Are you cruel? Do you chain them and have your will of them?'

She was breathing fast, her breasts rising and falling, never so aroused as when she was with soldiers. Male, female: it made no odds to her.

'You want me to show you?'

'Oh, yes!'

Now certain that she was about to have her

fantasies fulfilled, Isobel moved eagerly into Antonia's arms, thirsting for that first kiss. Their lips met and she could feel her lover's moving over hers, seeking, kissing first the corners then the full centre before opening them with her slippery tongue. Isobel surrendered her mouth, sighing deeply and winding her own tongue with Antonia's. She longed to feel those sensual lips sucking her breasts, then parting her labia and licking her, bringing her to bliss.

Antonia lifted her head and looked down at her. 'Is this what you want?'

'You know it is, but pretend I'm your prisoner.' Isobel's groin was tight with tension, a spasm of lust clenched like a coiled spring in her depths.

Antonia smiled and rolled her thumb over a nipple. Isobel arched her spine and pressed closer. 'Ah, yes…' she sighed, then flinched away, withdrawing to the far side of the bed, one arm folded over her breasts, the other hand cupping her pubis. 'Leave me alone,' she shouted. 'You're my enemy. How dare you touch me in so intimate a manner?'

Antonia indulged her, standing by the four-poster, hands on her hips, legs apart to balance her weight. 'Don't act the coy virgin with me, lady,' she sneered, adopting the role of a lecherous mercenary heated by blood-lust.

She yanked at the curtain cords and then wound her fingers in Isobel's hair, using it as a halter to drag her close. Isobel could smell her own arousal and any pretence of resistance crumbled as she was overwhelmed by the heat laving her core. Antonia gripped her tightly, then flipped her over on her back, held her arms widespread, slipped a loop of silk cord over each wrist and tied her securely to the posts on either side of the bed-head.

'So, milady? What now?' she asked. 'Are you ready to be tupped?'

For an instant she hovered, just above Isobel's breasts, and then lowered her head. Her hair fell forward, tickling the nipples and Isobel cried out as Antonia's tongue flicked them into stiff points. Pleasure broke over her, gathering force, her thighs wet with juice trickling from her sex. It was wonderful to feel so helpless, unable to defend herself against her own rampant desires.

Antonia ran her hand over the curves and hollows of Isobel's body, familiarising herself with the rounded belly, the alabaster thighs and dimpled knees. Then she took more cords and holding Isobel's legs wide apart, tethered her ankles to the elaborately carved foot-posts.

Now she was indeed a prisoner. She felt a frisson of fear, an adrenaline rush that almost tipped her over into orgasm. Antonia left her for a moment, sitting on a chair and hooking a toe at the heel of her boot, prising it off. The second followed, then the white woollen hose. She shrugged her shoulders out of her shirt and stood up, facing Isobel full on. Slowly, letting every movement tell, she unbuttoned the front flap of her breeches and let them fall, kicking them away when they reached her feet.

She had beautiful legs with long, pure lines. Her narrow hips and the supple slenderness of her waist added to the impression of aristocratic elegance. But Isobel could not take her eyes off the fascinating triangle at her fork. It stood out prominently, seeming swollen with female sexuality. The inky curls did not hide her cleft, deeply and sharply defined, offering itself to her gaze.

The breasts, the hips, the flanks and buttocks were

an all-over coppery hue, for she lay naked in the sun whenever she could. And the fullness of her mound was sensual, thrusting itself forward so invitingly that Isobel felt as if her own private places had been probed.

She knew that she had to be possessed and then possess that wonderful furrow. She wanted it open for her exploration, the plump lips and the hard pleasure nubbin rising from its cowl in response to her caresses.

As if attuned to her longings Antonia parted the hairy wedge and provoked her miniature bud, making it stand, flushed a deep pink. She rested one foot on the bed, stretching wide, granting Isobel a view of those subtle wet folds. She drew her forefinger along them, the top knuckle slightly bent as she crooked it under the head of her clitoris, rubbing it several times, and then withdrawing.

Leaning over, she trailed the finger over Isobel's lips and she sucked it in, tasting the strong essence, so reminiscent of her own. Then Antonia's mouth found hers, her tongue diving in again, sipping the honey-sweet dew of her saliva while Isobel made mewling noises deep in her throat.

Antonia rolled away, taking up a black silk scarf from the dressing-table and saying, 'Time for the blindfold. My prisoner mustn't know where she is or she may betray me.'

Isobel did not resist, and Antonia's hands were firm but gentle on her face as she placed the scarf round her eyes, reaching behind to knot it, catching strands of her hair. This was an exciting game and one of which Isobel never tired, almost painfully aroused by the fact that her other senses were sharpened when sight was denied her. She was transformed into a

10

being aware only of touch, taste and smell, and her ears seemed to be animal keen, picking up the smallest sound.

For a moment there was absolute silence. Then she heard the hiss as resin oozed from the burning logs, a horse cantering by outside, the creak of a floorboard close by. The mattress sagged as Antonia rejoined her, and Isobel waited breathlessly. She could smell her, skin tingling at her closeness, but still she jumped when fingers lightly grazed over her right nipple.

They left her, and it was as if she was alone again. Her skin was growing cold, a draught playing over it. Had Antonia abandoned her? Would she have to remain spread-eagled like that till her maid appeared in the morning? Indignation rose and she almost cried out, then heard a rustling and felt a touch – not fingers, but something soft being smoothed over her belly.

She stabbed a guess at its identity. It was a glove – one of her own white kid gloves. The feeling was sublime, heightening in intensity as the nap slid over the insides of her thighs, was passed across her mound and contacted the hair fringing her nether lips. Isobel moaned her desire to have it titillating her aching nubbin. She twisted her hips, lifted her pubis as high as she could given her restraints, begged for this blessing.

The glove was removed.

Fingers tweaked her nipples with a firmness that made her gasp. These were followed by lips, sucking, nibbling, an almost unendurable torment when she wanted them on her clitoris. Her captor refused to satisfy it. Utterly helpless and at her mercy Isobel could do nothing to relieve her frustration.

11

'You want me to free you?' Antonia asked. 'You have only to say the word.'

Isobel shook her head, but then her body convulsed and her flesh cringed in reaction to the cold bite of steel. The point of Antonia's dagger touched her pubis, kissed its way along the top of her pubic triangle, circled the dimple of her navel and caressed each nipple.

Now the menace of the poniard gave way to plush pile. Starting at her toes it whispered over her instep, glided past her knee and smoothed her inner thigh, brushed against her mons veneris. Antonia moved it slowly with a delicate, highly erotic touch. She parted the outer lips and the moist inner pair, and allowed it to toy Isobel.

Isobel's breathing was ragged, her skin flushed. Orgasm was so very close, but her bud needed a steady rubbing to make it explode in pleasure. She never doubted that it would happen, eventually. Antonia knew exactly what she needed. This was simply a tease to add to her excitement.

As if reading her mind Antonia slipped a finger into her vagina. It clasped that welcome digit and Isobel writhed on it blissfully, twin points of sensation raising her to the edge of ecstasy as a thumb pressed down on the clitoris stem.

Antonia moved. The bonds were released, the band whipped from Isobel's eyes and she was turned so that she lay with her head between her lover's thighs, her own legs open. The first touch of Antonia's tongue was enough to drive her to the brink, and her hips thrust forward to meet the next wet caress. She linked her arms round Antonia's body and pulled her closer. She could see her avenue, smell the odour of arousal, opening her mouth and extending her tongue

12

to lick Antonia's sex.

The sucking sensation of Antonia's mouth on the pulsing nub made her moan. Locked in a circle of passion they licked and kissed and probed each other's secret places. Isobel could feel the glorious waves of orgasm building inside her. A tingling began at her toes, shooting up her thighs and gathering in her loins. She groaned as the moment came ever closer. The sensations became more acute, rippling through her and then taking her to the pinnacle, consumed by a violent climax. Antonia was gasping with excitement, bucking against Isobel's tongue and pushing her pubis downwards as she, too, reached her crisis.

Antonia brought Isobel to earth quietly, and they lay side by side, pressed close and touching from shoulder to thigh, hands clasped tightly. Isobel closed her eyes as the last sweet spasms passed through her. Finally Antonia heaved up on one elbow and smiled into her face. She bent forward to kiss her, tasting herself on her lips. It was a soft kiss, a gentle, trusting kiss between lovers who know exactly how to pleasure one another.

'Welcome home, my warrior,' Isobel sighed.

'I've brought a comrade along.' Antonia hugged her and then released herself to sit on the side of the bed, calling out, 'You can come in now, Jamie.'

The door opened and a slim, good-looking young man stepped inside. 'At last!' he exclaimed with a broad smile. 'I've been listening to your groans of pleasure and look what it has done to me!' He displayed the front of his breeches, their fit distorted by the long line of his swollen penis beneath. 'Ladies, have pity on me.'

'Come. Join us. This is Lady Isobel, who has been

13

wanting to meet you.' Antonia held out her arms and he almost fell into them, kneeling on the floor between her legs. Isobel was delighted, having seen him from afar and expressed her interest to Antonia, never expecting that she would organise this treat. 'Isobel, this is Sir James Westbury, an important officer in my army. A dashing, fearless solider.'

Now he stood there, wearing all the apparel of a Cavalier, but this didn't remain on him for long. Antonia helped him to take off his doublet and his bell-sleeved shirt, displaying a broad, muscular chest lightly coated with brown hair. It matched the long curls that fell to his shoulders. He sat beside Antonia and prised off his boots and white stockings, then untied the points below his knees and stood so that the women might view him as he lowered his breeches with provocative slowness. They both sat there staring as, gradually, his lower belly came into view, coated with more hair, and then his cock, fully erect.

It was a matter of seconds before he was on the bed, demanding, 'Which one of you wants it first?'

'Isobel is our hostess. I'll watch while you thrust into her, but don't spend. I want my share too,' Antonia instructed.

He smiled down at Isobel, a delightful bed companion. Women might be her preferred sex but there was nothing like a solid shaft of flesh to finish the feast, and Isobel was nothing if not greedy, determined to experience every bodily sensation.

He was all that could have been wished for, controlled in spite of his arousal, plunging in and out of Isobel but withdrawing before it was too late, letting Antonia have the benefit of his rock hard tool. But it was Isobel who finally received his emission

14

when, driven beyond control he came at last, his spasms flooding her. She sighed, more than content, Jamie's weight pinning her down while her fingers were linked with Antonia's.

Chapter 1

I hate him, Judith thought, seething with resentment. I know it's wrong of me to feel like this but I can't help it.

He's loathsome to me – his presence, his voice, his smell – his *touch*. I can't bear him anywhere near me, yet I'm compelled to endure him, night after wretched night while he uses my body for his selfish gratification.

She lay flat on her back, staring up at the tester dimly illumined by firelight. The object of her detestation, her husband Steven, had rolled away from her as soon as his lust was satisfied. Judith had awaited his arrival, as on almost every night since her marriage, waited in fear, trepidation and revulsion so strong that it amounted to nausea.

She had heard his footsteps outside the door, seen him enter in his long nightshirt, watched from under lowered lids as he knelt in prayer by the bedside, then steeled herself for the moment when he would throw back the quilt and slither under the covers beside her. As usual he had lifted her robe, inserted his knee between hers, and then rammed his swollen penis into her dry, unwilling sex. A few thrusts, a groan, and he had slumped on her, spent, this the sole sum of his lovemaking. She had remained rigid throughout, and now felt his rapidly cooling emission sticky on her thighs.

The bedchamber had grey stone walls softened by the occasional arras, and was lit by a solitary candle. The smouldering logs glowed fitfully in the heart of the massive carved fireplace. Portraits of her husband's forebears stared down with jaundiced eyes from yellowing canvases. It seemed that they disapproved of Judith, always had since the day he brought her to Ferris Mead as a bride of fifteen.

Three years ago now, a match arranged by her parents with property, land and religion as prime importance. She had not been consulted, her feelings of no consequence, and had become the chattel of this stern man who was twice her age. She had shrunk from him on the wedding night. His possession of her had been nothing more than rape. No one had informed her what to expect and, apart from witnessing copulation in the barnyard, she had been entirely ignorant of what took place between a man and a woman. It had horrified her and turned her to ice.

The war had come as a blessing in disguise. Steven went off to fight but, despite her most un-wifely prayers, always returned. She did not know much about the events that had plunged the country into civil war, hearing a one-sided, garbled version when he and other neighbouring squires met. It had been dragging on, a savage conflict between the king and Parliament that split England in two. Lord Steven Ashley was for the rebels, and as feudal lord enlisted able-bodied men from the village, equipping and training them at his own expense.

When Judith ventured a question or two she was told to be quiet; she had enough to occupy her mind

16

with caring for the household and indoor servants, minding the stillroom, the kitchen, the dairy, performing her duties as lady of the manor. She must leave such weighty matters as war and politics to her betters – her brothers, father and husband, all well-established landowners and squires.

The first time Steven marched out at the head of his troops she had known a blissful lightness of heart. He was going into danger, for the king's men were mostly aristocrats well-versed in the strategies of battle. She could not pray for her husband's safety, weighed down with a sense of sin because she longed to be free of him. But it seemed that he led a charmed life, returning with hardly a scratch, entering her bed and forcing himself on her, totally unconcerned because she shrank from him.

He expected her to accept copulation as a duty, and was becoming increasingly demanding and angry because she was not yet pregnant. He was desperate for an heir. Now she pretended to be asleep and he was already snoring. Slowly and surreptitiously, burning up with frustration, she slid a hand into the neck of her nightgown and gently stroked one of her nipples.

It hardened into a peak and a sharp, pleasurable sensation shot down into her lower belly, culminating between her legs. Steven turned away from her, occupying his side of the bed, and she was encouraged to increase the caresses she was lavishing on her breasts. He must be asleep. It was safe for her to go on, secretly bringing herself to that state of ecstasy which she had discovered not long ago.

For months she'd been tormented with vague yet pressing desires that gathered in her secret folds. The need grew to examine them and explore the warm, damp place which it seemed no one must see or touch, save her husband. Even he did not look at her, always invading her body under the cover of darkness. For her part she was ignorant of that solid bar of flesh with which he penetrated her. She was not encouraged to feel him or allowed to see his shaft and balls. Their mating took place hurriedly, as if to be performed not for pleasure but for procreation. Judith had been certain there must be more to it than that.

Last time he was away she had indulged her curiosity about her body. One moonlit night she locked the bedroom door and stripped naked. Greatly daring she lit several candles and placed them around the mirror on its stand in the centre of the dressing-table. She had seen herself reflected there, never before realising that she was beautiful.

Long flaxen hair which, unpinned, flowed over her shoulders and halfway down her back, a slim body but with full breasts crowned by nipples as succulent as berries, a little waist, flat belly, long legs and graceful feet. But above all her eyes had been drawn to the fair triangle at the apex of her thighs. This was the place of mystery, these full lower lips fringed with curling hair and the dark slit between.

Judith had been unable to stop herself from examining it, spreading her legs and gently parting her crack. She had been unprepared for the pleasure that darted through her, centring on that tiny nub hardening at the very top of her labia. Someone other than herself had seemed to possess her. Holding the lips open she concentrated on this spot that had proved to be the fulcrum of desire. Driven by instinct she rubbed it with her middle finger, feeling it swelling, and the juice that seeped from that place which Steven insisted on violating.

Lost to the world she gently wetted her finger and passed it over her bud. The feelings this caused were sensational. She had been afraid of their intensity, sure that she was about to die yet unable to resist the waves of orgasm that flooded through her.

I'll be damned to hell, she had thought. Something so wonderful is bound to be forbidden and wicked. But no matter what she was unable to stop bringing herself to climax several times, each sharper and more intense than the last. Since that magical moment she'd grown bolder, wanting to see her genitals and witness the hardening of her nubbin.

A hand-mirror had provided the answer and many a night she squatted on the floor, holding it beneath her and observing her private parts; the two pairs of lips, the outer ones hair-fringed, thick and protective, the inner pink and soft and damp, the opening below where silvery liquid gathered, a perfect lubricant for that fleshy little kernel kept hidden by its cowl at the very apex of her crack. She examined her anus, too, pressing a finger against that tight opening which was reluctant to yield.

Now, lying in the four-poster beside her husband, the need to bring herself to climax was driving out all other thought. She scrunched up her nightgown till the hem was above her triangle and worked her clitoris with a gentle motion, feeling it swell. Very softly she caressed the aching head of it, then held back, practised in the ways of delaying orgasm, making it last. She fingered it carefully, rubbing each side of that straining little organ, tracing it back to where it was rooted firmly in her pubic bone.

It was quite large, maybe an inch from base to tip, but concealed by its membrane. Only the eager pearly-pink head was displayed. She yearned to massage it until she peaked. She had forgotten Steven existed, and with her free hand pushed her breasts together so she could reach both nipples, her thumb busy on one, her fingers on the other, her clitoris echoing the sweet torment of bodily need. Ecstasy warmed her from top to toe and she could not stop, leaving her breasts to concentrate, one hand holding her labia apart, the other finger flying over her nub.

It was coming. She could feel that exquisite pleasure gathering in her loins, ready to swamp her with delirious release.

'Yes… yes!' she whispered.

Then she was snatched rudely back from the brink of paradise.

'What are you doing?' Steven shouted, rearing up, his eyes blazing.

'Nothing… nothing,' she blurted out, hurriedly removing her hands and covering her nakedness.

'Lying slut! You were playing with yourself,' he thundered, disgust etched on his face. 'Wanton, filthy hussy! How dare you toy with your privates? Don't you know it's a grievous sin? How did you discover such a thing? Who has been teaching you? Was it one of the maids? Tell me, and I'll dismiss her at once.'

'No one showed me. I'm young and lusty. D'you expect me not to be hot? You have never, ever given me pleasure,' she cried, heedless of her words, knowing that he would punish her anyway.

'You're a lady,' he snarled, rigid with indignation. 'Brought up to be pious and demure. What's wrong with you? What flaw lies in your nature that you should even think of carnal pleasure?'

'I don't know about such things,' she retorted, sitting up and buttoning the neck of her gown. 'It's not as if I'm committing adultery. Surely there's no harm in my seeking satisfaction?'

'Isn't there?' he said, his voice low and menacing. 'You've not yet conceived and it's said if a woman indulges in this vice it prevents her from becoming with child. Is this what's been happening, you putting your selfish, vile and unnatural lust before our need to beget a son?'

This was too much for Judith. She rounded on him, her eyes glittering like sapphires. 'What nonsense is this? You were married for ten years to your first wife, and she died barren. Have you ever considered that the fault may lay with you, sir?'

His blow took her by surprise. Her cranium hit the headboard with a crack and stars danced before her eyes. 'Foul-mouthed whore!' he yelled, almost deranged with fury. 'How dare you question my potency? It's you who are preventing conception… you… you bitch!' and he went on smacking her across the face, implementing each word with a blow.

She flung her arms up to protect herself, then launched into him, hand connecting with his nose in a punishing swipe. Out of bed now and hopping with rage, 'Leave me alone, you bastard!' she stormed.

'Ha! You're my wife to do with as I please,' he shouted back, holding his damaged nose and glaring at her. 'Defy me, would you? A lewd trull who gets pleasure by rubbing herself between the legs, a trick only employed by base-born strumpets. Maybe you're a witch too, and are deliberately stopping my seed from entering your womb. Shall I turn you over to the village elders for examination? If they find you guilty they'll hang you.'

Terror made her knees weak. She had once seen how these so-called godly people treated someone

21

accused of witchcraft. She had been old, a wise-woman of the woods who never did any harm, but a case had been made against her and she was ducked in the river, the concept being that if she drowned she was innocent, if she did not, then it proved she was a witch. When they dragged her from the water she was dead. Innocent? She hadn't stood a chance either way.

'There's no need to be so angry, husband,' Judith said, though despising her cowardice. 'I swear to you I'm doing nothing to stop conceiving. I would like a baby too, you know.'

'Then why are you so perverse?' he went on, unprepared to climb down. 'You don't behave as a wife should. At times I fear that you neither love nor respect me.'

'That's not true,' she lied, wanting nothing but this violent scene to end.

'Why were you stroking yourself?' he said, and came closer to her, then seized her wrists in his, his fingers digging into her flesh like talons. 'Am I not man enough for you?'

She wanted to say that men had never interested her. Unlike her contemporaries who thought of nothing but marriage and children and obeying their husbands, she found the restraints imposed irksome and the opposite sex alarming. And as for that weird ritual between the sheets? It meant nothing to her. Steven neither provided her with the smallest iota of pleasure or inspired her with desire.

'You protect me, I know,' she prevaricated, turning her face away, disliking the odour of his breath.

'I do indeed. What d'you think my riding off to battle is all about if it isn't to safeguard you and Ferris Mead? What more would you have me do?'

22

'Nothing, nothing. You're right. I'm ungrateful, but I assure you that what you discovered me doing does no harm in any way. Now, please let me go. I need to use the chamber-pot,' she said.

His smile darkened and the look in his eyes was frightening. 'Let you go, so you can explore your cunny when I'm asleep? Oh no, my dear wife. You'll spend the rest of the night tied up. I'll give you no chance to rub yourself.'

He jerked her hands round behind her, pulled off one of the curtain cords and lashed it round her wrists, drawing it tightly and tying the ends to the bedpost.

'Don't, that hurts,' she protested, but he ignored this, fetched over the candle and pulled up her nightgown. Placing the light where it shone on her mound he dropped to his hunkers in front of her, and reaching up pushed his fingers into her bush, easing apart the labia and forcing her clitoris into prominence.

'Is this it?' he asked, his voice thick with excitement. 'Is this the thing you were fondling?'

'Yes,' she gasped, and even though she hated him she could not control the spasm that warmed her as he tickled it.

'You'd like me to go on?' he said, continuing that exciting frottage, and she could see the lust in his eyes.

'Yes, please,' she breathed jerkily. Was it possible that he might give her what she wanted so desperately?

'What does it feel like?' he whispered, and pinched her clit-head so hard that she nearly came and emptied her bladder at the same time. Instead she hung on and did neither.

23

'I can't describe it. Perhaps it's what you feel when you spend in me,' she ventured, gyrating her hips against his fingers.

'Evil-tongued trollop!' he roared and leapt to his feet. 'I'll not encourage your lechery.'

'Untie me, please,' she begged, fearing him as never before.

'No. You'll spend the rest of the night tethered like a wild beast,' he scoffed, all the bullying cruelty of his nature revealed.

'Please, I need to pass water,' she pleaded, the ache in her bladder superseding all else.

'You can't. I won't let you. You'll stay bound till morning,' he said, and resumed his place in bed, adding, 'If you can't control it and wet the mattress, then you'll be forced to clean it up when daylight comes.'

Judith stood on the battlements, looking out over the estate. Steven had been absent for a week, obeying his colonel's orders and harassing the enemy outposts near Oxford. She had heard him say that the king, having lost London, had set up his headquarters in the university town, and that the rebel forces nibbled away at it like terriers on the scent of rats. Though Ferris Mead was several miles away, he and his men went wherever they were directed.

A flush spread to her cheeks. She had not yet recovered from the humiliation Steven had heaped upon her, driven by spite and fear of losing control over her. The night had been long and she chilled to the marrow. She had not given him the satisfaction of voiding her bladder, clinging on painfully till she was untied at daybreak. But the iron had entered her soul. She would never forgive him.

24

She paced the walkway, then leaned against the parapet and gazed down into the courtyard below. The servants, going about their chores, were reduced to doll size. Their voices reached her clearly and she took deep breaths of sweet spring air. The smell of poultry runs and cow byres was carried on the breeze and smoke gusted from nearby chimneypots. It was early evening, the shadows lengthening as the sun sank.

Beyond the walls of this house that had once been a fortress the fields stretched out like a patchwork quilt, bordered by the green of copse and woodland. Every acre for leagues belonged to Steven.

Judith shaded her eyes and stared at the ribbon of road that wound into the distance. Strands of hair escaped from her white cap and blew into her mouth. Her attention sharpened. She caught the glint of armour, then the flash of a white and red banner. A cloud of dust arose from under horses' hooves. The cavalrymen had been recruited from among the squires and, like the company of foot soldiers, they wore the Ashley colours.

Details of the cavalcade sharpened as it advanced. Judith stepped backwards from the parapet, gathered up her skirts and headed for the rickety ladder that connected the roof to the next floor. Steven was home and would expect her to be at the front door to welcome him.

'The master's returned,' she informed Mrs Moffat, the housekeeper, as she swept down the stairs and into the Great Hall.

'I know, my lady. The houseboy came running in just now. He's been keeping watch on Brendan Tor. I've told Mr Barnes and he's ordered the servants to stand in line outside, save for the kitchen staff, of course. They'll be too busy preparing food for our brave lads.'

'Thank you, Mrs Moffat,' Judith said crisply, hackles rising. The sheer efficiency of the woman made her feel surplus to requirements. But then, Mrs Moffat had been Steven's housekeeper for years, certainly since the death of the first Lady Ashley.

Judith straightened her dress. It was dark brown wool, with a waist slightly higher than her normal one and a modest neckline trimmed with plain linen like the turned back cuffs of her full, elbow-length sleeves. Vanity and delight in frivolous attire was not encouraged and, though the mistress, Judith's gown was no finer than Mrs Moffat's.

She had the distinct feeling that the woman did not much like her. She was always deferential but with a hint of mockery, forever making small suggestions and issuing orders that somehow managed to countermand Judith's, though she was never downright rude. Judith knew the maids lived in fear of Mrs Moffat's harsh tongue and the cane she always carried. Judith had sometimes surprised an odd expression on the gaunt, middle-aged woman's face when she was chastising one of the girls. It was almost as if she was enjoying it.

The idea caused Judith a spasm of unease. How would it feel to bend over, lift her skirts and have the rod lashing down on her bare posterior? The girls concerned wept and squealed and made a great fuss, but there was a frenzied quality about their protests, as if there was more to it than pain.

Judith paced out beneath the arch of the massive main entrance and stood at the head of a wide flight of shallow stone steps. Below was a semi-circular gravelled area that led from the drive. The servants were ranged in order of importance to greet their lord, headed by Mrs Moffat and Mr Barnes.

There was an air of anticipation. Not much happened in the sleepy village of Lampton. The war had provided more excitement than most of the inhabitants had had in a lifetime. While not actually facing the enemy, those left behind had the entire fret and worry as loved ones marched off to fight, the anxieties about husbands and sons, the joy if they returned, the sorrow should they not.

Judith knew that soon a crowd would begin to gather and Steven would order food, small ale and cider to be distributed among his workers and tenant farmers. The way his troop carried themselves suggested that, though bone-weary, they had been successful. They waved to friends along the way, each man adopting a swagger as if they were hardened mercenaries, not yokels whose only weapon had once been a scythe, not a musket or pike.

Steven rode at their head, and behind him Judith saw a stranger who sat proudly in the saddle, a wide-brimmed hat set at a jaunty angle on curling dark hair. A black cloak hung from the rider's shoulders and draped the thigh-high leather boots and the withers of the thoroughbred that tossed its mane, snorted and rolled its eyes.

A groom ran to Steven when the cortege halted, holding the bridle while he dismounted. He turned to the stranger and his voice rang out across the sudden hush.

'You may get down, but don't try any tricks.'

The stranger spread wide gloved hands and said, with a wry smile and a shrug, 'Tricks, sir? And what tricks would these be? I've already surrendered my sword.'

'That's true, and you're my prisoner. I shall obey the code of war and you'll be unharmed, providing you behave yourself. Now, come inside and I'll arrange for your accommodation.'

Steven took the steps two at a time and stopped when he reached Judith. She dipped into a curtsey, saying, 'Welcome, my lord,' but managing to take a peep at the prisoner.

For some reasons she could not name a thrill swept through her, and a heightening of perception. This was a Cavalier, one of the king's followers who had the reputation for being recklessly brave, but wild and licentious, too.

Her fleeting glance showed this captured Royalist to be young and handsome, a tall, spare person who, though travel-stained, retained a haughty posture and was more finely clad than any of Steven's men, wearing a leather buff coat over his doublet, to protect him from sword thrusts and bullets.

'My wife, Lady Judith,' her husband said.

The stranger swept her ironic bow, saying, 'Your servant, madam.'

'And this is...' Steven began, but the Cavalier broke in.

'Captain Durward.'

Steven rounded angrily, almost shouting, 'You may call yourself captain but this can never be. You're not a proper soldier.'

Captain Durward laughed. 'And why not, sir? Didn't my men and I give you a hard fight before you captured me? I enlisted at the onset of war. Prince Rupert is my commander and, like you, I finance my brigade.'

They walked into the hall with a handful of Steven's officers. Judith was puzzled by the way in which both he and his friends were looking at Durward. They were suspicious and wary, hands resting on sword hilts as if they expected to be attacked at any moment. Yet Durward did not seem aggressive, and was unarmed, outnumbered and a prisoner.

'I'll confine you in one of the guestrooms,' Steven said, staring at his captive, perplexed. 'You'll be well treated and will write to the prince to this effect and tell him that I hold you as hostage. He has several of our men in captivity, and we can bargain for their release. But there's one condition.'

'And what is that?' Durward replied calmly, eyes resting on Judith, a tiny flame, like a jet of amber, shining in the depths of peat-dark eyes.

'Your attire, of course, Lady Antonia. I know who you are. Your reputation has preceded you. You are, in fact, somewhat notorious,' Steven sneered. 'However, I can't allow a woman to live in my house dressed as a man. You'll be supplied with more suitable garments.'

Now suddenly all the pieces of the puzzle slotted into place and Judith stared at the prisoner open-mouthed. A woman? A she-soldier? Astonishment was followed by an immediate stab of envy. How grand to be free of hampering skirts, able to ride astride a horse and, more important still, escape from the yoke of matrimony. As she examined Antonia's face she could now see that she was looking at a beautiful woman not a handsome man. The fire and force of her took Judith's breath away. She wanted to be like her.

'My lord, you seem to imagine that this may cause me some hardship,' Antonia said, her voice low and amused. 'I can assure you this isn't so. I'm perfectly accustomed to donning gowns, if and when it suits me, but this would hardly be practical when I'm riding at the head of my troopers or taking part in military activities. I'm sure you can see the sense in this.'

Steven's face darkened. He was obviously extremely uncomfortable in the presence of this powerful female. She spoke out boldly, courteous but firm, and Judith's admiration increased.

'You shouldn't even be considering going into battle, and living in camps among the rough soldiers,' Steven spluttered. 'It's most unseemly and an abomination. Why, you're no better than a camp-follower!'

Antonia took off her hat and ran a hand through her curls, her generous mouth curving in a smile as she answered, 'And what, my lord, is your concept of camp-followers?'

'Everyone knows they are women of loose morals who hang around the armies offering themselves for money, and indulging in lechery and fornication,' he shouted, his face turning beet-red.

Antonia perched herself on a corner of the refectory table, one leg braced on the floor, the other swinging lightly. 'This may be so in Roundhead camps, but in our army they mostly consist of wives and sweethearts who have gone with their men to cook for them, wash their shirts, darn their socks and tend them if they're wounded or sick. Of course there are and always will be women who, on the demand of men, make a living out of letting them use their bodies, and I suspect this also happens on your side. But on the whole camp-followers assist the army, invaluable as victuallers, nurses, and comforters.'

'Then why were you not content in this role?'

Steven demanded, while his officers watched silently.

'Because I had other skills. I could shoot and use a sword. As Countess of Heathleigh I had the wherewithal to form my own company of soldiers, women as well as men. Oh yes, I'm not the only one, and it pleases me to do so, my lord. I'll bow the knee to no one save my king.'

'And your husband?'

'I'm not married, nor will be until such time as it suits me.'

'May God forgive you for your arrogance!'

Antonia's smile deepened as she said, 'Oh, I'm sure He or She will. I'm on comfortable terms with the Almighty. I've had to be, so often staring death in the face.'

'You blaspheme!' he hissed, and swung round on the heel of his boot, shouting, 'Sergeant Linsey, take this woman upstairs. Mrs Moffat will show you the way.' Then he turned back to Antonia, saying, 'Do I have to chain you or will you give me your word not to try and escape?'

Antonia considered him slowly, one eyebrow raised, then answered, 'My word, sir? As an officer and a gentleman? Or as a woman?'

'Just give it,' Steven blustered. 'I don't want to have you manacled.'

'Don't you?' Antonia said and sauntered casually after Mrs Moffat, a beefy, red-faced sergeant on one said, his aide on the other. 'Now what makes me think that you'd rather enjoy it? Maybe it's the meekness of your wife. She looks browbeaten. What have you been doing to her, my lord?'

'Take her away!' he stormed. 'I've never known such a brazen female! Ye gods, is this the sort of person King Charles chooses to serve him? No

31

wonder you're losing the war.'

Antonia ignored this, but her eyes met Judith's and lingered.

Now Antonia winced as she shrugged her shoulder out of her cloak and dropped it on to the bed. Alone, she allowed herself to feel the tiredness, the pain, the fury with herself for a stupid mistake that had separated her from the others. Had she been more alert she'd not have been surrounded and captured.

It had been such an unimportant skirmish. At dawn she had led a party to a bridge to prevent the rebels crossing. A simple manoeuvre that should have been accomplished without bloodshed on either side.

Her heart sank as she realised that such attacks were happening with increasing frequency lately. Back in August, 1642, the Royalists had been confident that they would beat the enemy by December, the king restored to his palace in London and the troubles over. It hadn't happened that way. Two years down the line and there was a new man in charge, Oliver Cromwell, who was modelling his army on Prince Rupert's when it came to cavalry charges.

Antonia eased off her doublet, noting the blood staining it. Her shirtsleeve bore a wet, crimson patch. Through the torn linen she could see a gash where she'd taken a sword thrust in the upper arm. This was hours ago now and the wound had stiffened. She sat down on the joint stool before the dressing-table and unbuttoned her shirt, stripping to the waist. The cut was clean, but it needed to be sutured to heal neatly. She wondered if there was a surgeon in Ashley's platoon.

He seemed civilised enough, though she had been

struck by the pale face and scared eyes of his wife. There was obviously no love there. Lady Judith appeared to be petrified of him.

Rising she prowled the room, looking for a possible means of escape. There was no way she was going to stay there. Rupert must not be persuaded to treat for her freedom in exchange for that of Roundhead officers. She was not worried about her troop; her second-in-command, Jamie Westbury, would take care of everything. No doubt he was planning how they might find out where Antonia had been taken and organising a party of handpicked veterans to rescue her.

Just for now, however, she had to bite on the bullet and suffer the ignominy of being a prisoner. She ran her hands through her hair. She was dirty, smelly and needed to wash. Her stomach growled, her arm ached and it was hard not to despair; until now she had led a charmed life, neither captured nor injured.

'God dammit!' she muttered, gazing from the mullioned window. It was dusk, the birds wheeling above the treetops seeking night-time roosts.

The window was easily opened, but when she leaned out it was to look down a sheer drop. There was not a foot or handhold anywhere. Lord Ashley had chosen well when he selected this room as her prison.

She heard the key turn in the lock and swung round to see Judith coming in. She was carrying clothing.

'For you,' she said.

'Thank you,' Antonia replied, reaching her in a couple of strides. She took the garments, exclaiming, 'I would have preferred something more fashionable. Grey has never suited me.' She held the dress up, gazing in the mirror and pulling a face. 'How very unbecoming.'

'One of the housekeeper's,' Judith explained. 'You are of her height. Nothing of mine would have fitted you. In any case, I own nothing pretty... not the sort of thing to which you're accustomed, I'm sure.'

'Don't worry. These will do. I'd like to keep my buff coat, but is it possible that you might have my breeches, doublet and linen laundered?'

'Of course. I'll see to it, but oh, dear, you're hurt!' Judith exclaimed, and took a step towards her. 'Wait one moment,' and she ran to the door and gave an order to someone standing outside.

'Have you asked for hot water? I stink like a fiddler's bitch,' Antonia remarked, aware of her naked breasts and the way in which her nipples were crimping in the cool air. She saw Judith glance at them and then look away, a flush mounting to her cheeks.

'If you will permit it, your ladyship, I can bathe and bind your wound,' she murmured. 'And there's an unguent I've made of herbs that will soon make it better.'

'Quite the little goodwife, aren't you?' Antonia teased, then added, 'But not happy, I think.'

'There's more to life than happiness,' Judith flashed back at her. 'We're not put on this earth to enjoy ourselves.'

'Aren't we?' My God, here's a pious little Puritan, Antonia thought, and the poor creature doesn't mean a word of it.

A maidservant came in bearing a bucket of steaming water and some towels. Judith dismissed her and turned her attention to Antonia's injury. She poured a measure into the china basin on a side-table, tested it for temperature, then took up a cloth and said, 'Please be seated. I'll try not to hurt you.'

She was gentle but firm, ignoring Antonia when she swore as the wound was cleansed and the ointment applied. Finally it was covered with a fine white bandage and fastened in place.

'Thank you,' Antonia said. 'You make a splendid nurse.' In the midst of her pain she was aware of the closeness of Judith, the fragrance of her hair, the softness of her hands, the alchemy that was working like yeast between them. She was sure that Judith was as yet unaware. Her timid glances, her blushes betraying that this was the first time she had even considered the possibility that she might find a woman attractive.

'I enjoy caring for the sick,' she said timidly. 'The villagers sometimes come to me for help.'

'I could do with you as an assistant to my sawbones,' Antonio said, standing and, taking up the cake of soap, working lather over her bare breasts, her ribs and her armpits.

'I couldn't do that,' Judith protested, and Antonia felt her tremble as she handed her a towel. 'I don't know how you've had the courage… living rough, sleeping in the open, surrounded by danger.'

'You never know what you can do until you try,' Antonia responded, and ran a finger down the curve of Judith's cheek. The smoothness and delicacy of the skin caused a quiver to course along her nerves. She was filled with the desire to snatch her away from her stifling environment and show her the big wide world that existed beyond the walls of Ferris Mead.

'I can't try anything. I'm married to Steven and that's an end to it,' Judith averred, but she did not withdraw from Antonia.

'Have you children?'

'No. He blames me because I'm barren.'

'I see. Well, Judith, I hope we'll become friends. I'm not used to being cooped up and shall probably go mad with boredom.'

'I'll come when I can,' Judith said, and Antonia could see how nervous she was. 'Have you everything you want? The privy is through that door. I've included a nightgown among these things. Supper will be brought to you soon and breakfast served at seven o'clock.'

'I appreciate your kindness, Lady Judith,' Antonia answered, and suppressed the impulse to put her arms around her. One had to be so careful not to misread the signals, but she was convinced that this Puritan lady needed loving. Perhaps captivity would not be so boring after all.

Unable to believe that she was about to do something so reprehensible, Judith looked up and down the corridor, then darted into the bedroom next to Antonia's. She had discovered its secret during one of her explorations of the old house, never realising that it would prove useful to her.

The daylight was fading fast, but she made straight for the armoire built into the wall that separated the two chambers. It was empty, smelling faintly of lavender. She stepped inside and half closed the door and applied her eye to the chink at the back, once blocked by a knot of wood. She wondered yet again who had made this spy-hole and for what purpose. Her own was irresistible and crystal clear. She wanted to see more of Antonia, and she was not disappointed. The room was ablaze. Antonia must have taken the tinder-box to every candle there.

Judith's breath shortened and her heart pounded as she filled her eyes and senses with the sight of Antonia stark naked. Such a superb body, lithe and graceful, with golden-brown skin and those gorgeous breasts that Judith had wanted so much to touch earlier.

Antonia had one foot on the joint stool, the other on the floor as she ran a hand between her legs and washed herself there. Her pubis was darkly furred, the bush thick and luxurious, forming a perfect triangle. Having completed her ablutions Antonia dried carefully, but instead of picking up the nightgown that lay in readiness on the bed, she sat down on the edge of the mattress, thighs apart. One of her hands moved between her legs, sought a point further down and stayed there for a moment, and then it rose again, trailing along the groove in her flesh.

She repeated this action and Judith watched, fascinated, and lifted her hands to her breasts, impatient of their covering, tugging at the front lacing. It yielded and she cupped their roundness and circled her nipples with her thumb-pads. Sweet, suffocating anguish passed through them and shot down to her sex.

Antonia's finger toyed with her crack, the others raised gracefully until she came to rest on her clitoris. Judith's heart was hammering so hard she was afraid it would be heard. She passed her tongue over her dry lips while Antonia continued her private game, her finger pressing down more deeply, the tip hidden by her fleshy folds. Then she used her other hand to hold them aside. Her finger paused, circled her nub, patted and stroked it.

Judith was suffering acutely, ready to explode into orgasm as she lifted her skirt and found her own pleasure centre. Yet she wanted to delay the moment, to watch Antonia bring herself off and then enjoy her own climax.

The whole scene was a revelation to her. Till then she had imagined she was unnatural, Steven's accusations about what he called her 'solitary vice' convincing her that she was insane or worse. But now she was watching this magnificent woman enjoying herself in the same way. Judith was not abnormal. Women did this to themselves. Steven was wrong.

Antonia's movements became more frantic. Her eyes were half closed; her head tilted back, that mane of hair like a cape across her shoulders. Her breasts looked larger, the nipples hard as cob-nuts. She relaxed against the pillows and separated her pink folds.

Judith heard her moaning and saw the swiftness of her finger dancing over her swollen nub. Antonia's moan became a cry. Her thighs opened violently then snapped shut on her hand, imprisoning it. She fell back, panting. Judith gasped and came against her own finger, knees weak and her head swimming. Her eye was at the hole again, feasting on the woman lying on the bed and she wanted to go to her, embrace her, bury her face between those splendid thighs and declare the passion that blossomed inside her like a crimson rose.

Chapter 2

'This should have been stitched. I'll bear a scar, and this I shall lay at your husband's door.' Antonia glowered in the mirror as Judith attended to her wound.

'There is no surgeon here, I'm afraid.'

'Ha! And if there was what sort of bungler would that have been? A self-righteous rebel who might have done more harm than good! No thank you!'

She made Judith nervous, so angry at being imprisoned, restless and eager to get out. She had refused to breakfast with them at seven o'clock and a meal had been sent up to her room. Judith had come to administer to her before she dressed. The wound was healing well and would hardly have benefited from being sutured. However, she listened to Antonia grumbling, sympathising with her frustration.

'Shall we walk in the garden later?' she suggested. 'My husband has given his permission.'

'Very magnanimous of him,' Antonia sneered. 'And how long does he propose to keep me penned up?' Then her eyes softened, and she squeezed Judith's hand. 'Don't look so woeful. I know it isn't your fault.'

Her touch burned through Judith, a sharp reminder what she had witnessed and experienced the night before. Steven's closest contact had never moved her like this. She had always striven to avoid him. 'You must lead an exciting life,' she ventured, replacing the ointment and linen in her basket.

'I've always been happier riding and acting the tom-boy than learning to be a good housewife.' Antonia threw off her nightgown and stood there naked, stretching before she donned a chemise and petticoats, topped by the grey dress.

Judith had never witnessed such uninhibited behaviour, always taught to hide her body and be modest in all things for her family had been of the

Puritan persuasion, like Steven. Antonia resembled someone from another planet.

'And when are we to take this walk?' she asked, running a brush through her curling hair and making no attempt to pin it up or hide it under the white cap provided. She looked like a gypsy.

'This afternoon,' Judith answered, wishing they could go at that moment. She turned towards the door. 'I'll send a servant to fetch the washbowl,' and though loathe to leave, she couldn't get out fast enough.

Steven apprehended her in the Great Hall, fingers digging into her arm. He had been particularly brutal last night, forcing himself upon her, muttering, 'That brazen she-soldier may think herself equal to me, but I have something she never will – a cock,' and he thrust it into her with savage force, leaving her bruised and sore.

'What is it, husband?' Judith now asked, dragging herself free.

'Has she said anything, done anything?' He seemed obsessed with his prisoner. 'Keep your ears open. She may let some information drop. We need to know the movements of the Royalists and their intentions. Our side is growing ever stronger under the leadership of the new man, Cromwell.'

'You want me to act as a spy?' Judith resolved never to do so. She would do nothing to harm Antonia.

'Yes. She will be here some time. My messenger has gone into Oxford, but these matters are slow. Let her view you as a friend. Lower her guard. I have already said you can stroll in the grounds together, though Mrs Moffat will follow at a distance.'

'That black crow!' Judith was exasperated.

He frowned. 'She's a faithful servant, and will do as I tell her.'

And there lay the problem, Judith thought, and a plan was forming in her mind. She would organise Antonia's escape if possible, although the thought of never seeing her again was painful. Then the daring idea struck her like a lightning bolt. Why not go with her?

Her head was buzzing as she walked into the still-room where pickles and preserves rubbed shoulders with medicines and herbs. Dare she run from Ferris Mead? It was her home, no matter how unhappy. Without it she would have nothing, no money, and no shelter, even her dowry belonged to Steven. It would take a tremendous amount of courage or real desperation to leave it all behind. But the idea grew and blossomed, and developed even more strongly when she and Antonia walked in the garden.

She would like to have taken her arm, but this would have seemed too bold, and Mrs Moffat was following them at a respectful distance with gimlet eyes fixed upon their every movement.

'This is a lovely house,' Antonia remarked. 'It reminds me of my home, Heathleigh Hall in Wiltshire.'

'Do you miss it?'

'Naturally, but I manage to get back sometimes. It's not all marching and fighting, you know. There are gaps between battles, skirmishes and sieges, and armies can't move in the winter. The roads are too bad, deep in mud and impossible for the horses to pull artillery.'

'That's when Steven returns, and stays for a long while.' Judith did not try to hide the hardness in her voice when she mentioned his name. She found

Antonia so easy to talk to and within a short time had conveyed her feelings of resentment, though keeping her voice low, lest Mrs Moffat overhear.

'I'm sorry that you are so unhappy,' Antonia murmured, as they paced the gravelled path that connected with the stables. 'This is the fate of many wives, married young to a man they don't love.'

'I was told that love is not important in a union between two people who have the same expectations and religion. It is even looked upon as a bad thing, usually ending in tragedy.'

Antonia smiled at her. 'Maybe this is right. Love can do very strange things to one.'

'Have you ever been in love?' Judith had never before met anyone that she could converse with about such matters.

'I've had my moments of insanity.' Antonia's laughter rang out among the stone walls of the stable block, causing heads to turn as the outdoor staff went about their duties.

'Is that what you call it?' Judith was aware of Mrs Moffat glancing their way, attracted by the laughter. Her face was grim.

'Indeed. It's a state when one loses one's wits, able to think of nothing but the beloved.' Judith was surprised to see a wistful look on Antonia's face, but this passed quickly and she was smiling again. 'I prefer to be free of it, to enjoy myself with whom I please, but keep heart whole. Despite what I told your husband I shall marry some day in the hope of providing an heir for my estate. I was the only child, you see, and it belongs to me. But don't think I'll be bowing to a lord and master. I shall choose a man who will respect me and treat me as an equal.'

Antonia was like a breeze blowing through Ferris

Mead. Judith's head was spinning with concepts that she had never before thought possible. 'And is it true that you provide for your own soldiers?'

Antonia nodded. 'Like other members of the nobility I recruited men from my village. I've set up headquarters in the family house in Oxford. There's plenty of room, and grounds where tents can be erected. I've been joined by men and women who wanted to fight for the king, relishing the idea of freedom from the restrictions imposed upon them. I pay most of the expenses, for the Royalist finances are in confusion, and the Roundheads in possession of the mint, left behind when the king abandoned London for Oxford at the beginning of the conflict.'

'Why do you call them Roundheads?' This puzzled Judith.

Antonia chuckled. 'Because of their short haircuts. They despise the long locks of the Cavaliers.'

They were approaching the stables and Judith said, 'Would you like to see your horse?'

'I would. He's a fine beast, though it is wise not to fall in love with one's animal, any more than with a human. There's always a chance of losing it.'

'We're going to look at the horses, Mrs Moffat,' Judith said, finding that Antonia's presence gave her the courage to speak boldly.

'Very well, my lady,' she answered. 'I'll wait out here. Can't abide them myself, snappy creatures.'

It was dim inside and smelling sweetly of hay. A groom doffed his hat. 'Good afternoon, ma'am.'

Judith recognised him; indeed she had noticed him before. He was slim, brown-haired and around her age. He had an engaging smile. 'Ah, Tom,' she said, 'we want to see Lady Durward's horse.'

'That's him, over there.' Without hesitation

43

Antonia moved towards one of the stalls where a black stallion lifted his head and whinnied at the sound of her voice. She caressed his silky nose and flowing mane, crooning, 'Sultan, my beauty. Are they caring for you well? Don't fret. We'll ride together again very soon.'

'He's a fine one, ma'am,' said Tom, and he joined her in petting Sultan. 'But a handful to manage, I'll wager.'

'I can handle him. He's quiet as a lamb for me, even in battle.'

Tom's eyes widened. 'Do you really join in the fighting? They've been talking about you. Said you were a she-soldier. Is it true?'

'It is, Tom, and I'm not the only one. How is it you're not fighting?'

'I wanted to, but Lord Ashley says he needs some of us here to look after the place when he's off with his troop.' He looked over at Judith. 'I'm proud to do so, for I'd defend my lady to the death.'

His eyes spoke volumes, and Judith could feel the colour mounting to her face, while the thought sprang into her mind of how it would be if he took Steven's place in her bed.

'A noble paladin, I'm sure,' teased Antonia. 'And are you from these parts?'

'I don't know where I'm from, ma'am. I was a foundling, left on the steps of the church when newborn. The first Lady Ashley had me fostered by the head groom and his wife. They brought me up with their own. I took his name. I'm Thomas Maslin, ma'am.'

Judith listened, surprised. Antonia had managed to get more information about him in five minutes than she had in three years. Now she looked at him with fresh eyes. He was an attractive lad who must set hearts aflutter among the maidservants.

'And which army would you join, given the chance?' Antonia asked, still fondling Sultan.

'I don't know much about the war, only what the others say, that the king is a tyrant and that we have to fight to keep our freedom and practice our religion.'

'I think a strapping lad like you would fair better with my side,' Antonia murmured, and Judith noticed that she had moved closer to him, her shoulder against his as they leaned on the stall. 'We must talk more of this. Tomorrow afternoon, perhaps, when we come walking again.'

'Very well, ma'am. And will you be here as well?' He turned towards Judith and she nodded eagerly. Though taught not to hobnob with the servants, she wanted to see more of him.

'We did well this afternoon,' Antonia said later, when Judith came in to dress her wound. 'That young man will be useful.'

'How so?' Judith had been waiting impatiently for the time when she could be with Antonia again. Now, after supper, she would stay for a while, for Steven had gone to a meeting with the church elders.

'My dear child, can't you see that he's taken with you? I swear he'll be putty in your hands,' Antonia said, while Judith attended to her injury.

'So what if he is? I'm a married woman.'

'An unhappy one.' Suddenly Antonia put her undamaged arm around her and held her close. 'I'd so much like to see you sparkling with life, as you should be. You're beautiful, Judith. I could show you delights you've never dreamed of.'

Judith relaxed in her embrace, feeling she'd come home at last. Her mother had never shown her much affection, neither had her father or her siblings. She had seen little of them since her marriage, staunch Puritans who kept much to themselves. To be held as Antonia was doing made her want to cry at such a demonstration of warmth and feeling.

Overcome with emotion she tried to pull away. 'Don't say such things. You know it can never be.'

'Why not?' Antonia ran her lips over Judith's cheek and then her tongue circled her ear. Judith shuddered with delight.

'How can it happen? I'm tied to Steven and you are his prisoner.' But Judith's earlier thoughts of organising an escape were uppermost in her mind.

Now Antonia's hands were on Judith's breasts. Even though they were covered the sensation was intense, stabbing right down to her sex. 'Help me to get away.'

'But then I should never see you again.' Judith was unable to resist the wonderful feelings Antonia's kisses and touch were engendering.

'Come with me,' she breathed, close to Judith's mouth.

'Leave here, you mean?' This was almost too much for her to take in. Her dream was becoming reality.

'Yes, and we'll take Tom, too. I'm sure we can persuade him to aid us. He's already half in love with you. Give him a little encouragement and he will have horses ready, when we give him the word.'

'Can I do it? I want to. Oh yes, Antonia, I want so much to come with you. But I shall have nothing. Can you promise to shelter me, find me work to do, even teach me to fight?'

'Never fear. You have my word to do all these

46

things. I shan't abandon you, Judith,' and still holding her she eased towards the bed.

The room was dark, only the flickering fire and a pair of candles lit the gloom, and Judith felt as limp as a rag-doll, all her strength sapped by the incredible feelings that swamped her. At one moment she was aware that Mrs Moffat might come in, and in the next she didn't care.

Antonia laid her back among the pillows, still kissing and caressing her, then stretched out beside her. Judith tingled at the touch of her hand on her ankle, pushing up her skirt and petticoats and softly working its way higher, past her knees and towards her thighs.

'Oh, oh…' Judith breathed.

Antonia paused. 'You want me to stop?'

'No… no.'

The gentle exploration continued and now Judith was fully exposed, with Antonia bending over her and murmuring, 'What a lovely little cunt. It should be treated with reverence, not brutalised. Your husband sounds like a selfish monster.'

'I've never had anyone else,' Judith gasped, and Antonia's fingers came ever closer to her cleft, and then alighted on the prominent bud that crowned it.

'All men are not like him,' Antonia promised, parting Judith's vaginal lips and sliding a finger to her clitoris. 'I can assure you of this, for I make love to both sexes and find them equally enjoyable. Relax, dear heart, and let me bring you to bliss.'

Suddenly there was a loud knock on the door and Mrs Moffat shouting, 'His Lordship is home and demanding to see you, my lady!'

'I must go.' Judith scrambled up and adjusted her clothing. 'We'll talk more tomorrow. Goodnight,

Antonia.'

Her heart was hammering as she closed the door behind her, coming face to face with Mrs Moffat who looked at her in an enquiring way. She knew what lay ahead, Steven cross-questioning her about the prisoner while she lied and kept the secret to herself. Antonia and she were going to escape together, and she prayed that he would take his troop off soon, making this possible.

He was pacing the library, a black scowl making his face even harder. 'I gather you've been spending time with the prisoner,' he began, hardly giving Judith time to close the door.

'At your bequest, sir,' she answered spiritedly. 'Did you not instruct me to do so? Beside, I am attending to her wound.'

'I don't like your attitude,' he said coldly. 'I trust you're not learning her wanton ways.'

'And what, pray, are those?' She had never realised just how much she disliked him and all he represented.

'She's a Jezebel. Wearing breeches and riding astride and fighting, if you please. Thinking herself on an equal footing with her betters.'

'And who might they be?' Judith knew the answer, aware that she was playing with fire but no longer caring.

'You know very well who!' He was working himself into a rage. 'Men, of course! Women have their place, but it is in the home seeing to the wants of their husbands.'

Judith wished so much that Antonia was there. She was still frightened of him, but his words infuriated her. 'Men are not superior to us. We are equally capable of doing many of the things they look upon as their right.'

'Nonsense! You have your place in the scheme of things, but are definitely inferior. Get you to bed and I'll follow, and let us hear no more of this.'

Despising herself for her cowardice, Judith took a candle and lit herself up the stairs and into the master bedchamber. The four-poster seemed to crouch there like some malignant monster, scene of her humiliation and pain, and now she must share it with him again. She undressed reluctantly and slipped her nightgown over her head, and then she heard him enter the room and close the door behind him. There was no escape.

He grabbed her and flung her facedown across the quilt. She did not attempt to struggle, hoping he might be merciful if she was compliant. It was a vain hope. Steven was in an ugly mood, and she felt the air on her naked buttocks as he exposed them. This was followed by a swish and burning pain as his riding crop made contact with her skin.

'Defy me, would you? We'll see about that!' he muttered, and implemented his words with another blow.

Judith bit her lip to stifle her cries, unwilling to give him the satisfaction of knowing how much he was hurting her. It was not the first time he had chosen this method of punishment and, until lately, she had gone along with the general idea that a husband had every right to chastise his wife. But Antonia had made her think again, and the conclusion she had reached was that this was a pack of lies. Even so, at this moment she had no means of defending herself. Besides which she did not want to arouse his suspicions and make escape even more difficult, but each blow stiffened her resolve. Let him think he was subduing her. He'd soon learn different when she and Antonia had vanished.

Steven was getting into his stride, lust and the urge to bully combining to make him crueller than ever. He stood by the side of the bed in his shirtsleeves, his arm rising and falling, Judith's hinds crisscrossed with stripes from his repeated blows. She sobbed, burying her face in the pillows but stubbornly refusing to beg for mercy.

At last he flung the whip aside and plunged his cock into her unwilling flesh. She was dry and it hurt, but this added to his pleasure.

Judith endured, praying he would finish quickly, but he kept on and on, thrusting and withdrawing, muttering dirty words that he would never have admitted using in his daily life. She could hardly breathe, weighed down by his body, clenching her hands in the sheet beneath her and longing for him to reach his zenith and roll off her.

The thought came to her that maybe if she screamed and struggled this would excite him further and bring about a conclusion. 'Let me go, you're hurting me!' she cried, bucking against him.

'Oh no, you have to learn that I am master!' He grunted and his thrusts increased until at last she felt his final spasms and knew her ordeal was over.

He stretched on his side and the relief was intense. Judith pulled her nightgown into place, the soreness of her buttocks preventing her from resting on her back, and was even more determined that she and Antonia should escape.

'See what he did to me last night.' Judith lifted her skirts and displayed the marks on her buttocks.

Antonia winced. 'And this was done in anger, not to add to your pleasure?'

'Of course. He was furious with me for speaking out. How could it be pleasurable?'

'Never mind that now; though some people like to be dominated I can tell that this is not the case with you. Come here, sweetheart.' She took Judith into her arms. 'Poor child, it is high time you found a better life.'

'We'll plan to escape together, yes?' Judith no longer had any hesitation. 'And use Tom to help us.'

'Your part in this is to seduce him.' Antonia held her away a little and looked straight into her eyes. 'You want to, don't you? Don't tell me you haven't thought of making love with him, feeling that strong young body pressed close to yours, both mother-naked?'

It was impossible to deny. 'Yes,' Judith whispered, unsure if it was the picture this conjured or the feel of Antonia so close that caused this sudden wave of longing. 'But I couldn't, could I? Supposing I found myself with child?'

Antonia threw back her head and laughed. 'Well, you've not done so with your husband, and I can provide you with an unguent that I and many other ladies use to prevent conception. Come, let us lay plans and start putting them into operation this afternoon.'

It was then that she kissed her, and Judith melted. Never had she been kissed like that. Antonia's breath was sweet, her lips softly parting Judith's and her tongue gently exploring. Her embrace was wonderful, exciting yet comforting, too. If this was how kissing felt with a member of her own sex, then what would it be like with Tom? She couldn't wait to find out and spent the morning in a whirl, though trying to appear perfectly calm in front of Mrs Moffat and Mr Barnes, going about her duties with calm efficiency.

At last they were out in the sunshine, everything bursting into bloom and the birds in a frenzy of nest building. Judith's heart was light. The prison door was ajar and all it needed was the courage to push it open. Mrs Moffat trailed behind them, complaining that her feet ached and she would far rather be taking her afternoon nap. This was a good omen. Perhaps they could settle her down on a bench in the stable yard and she might drop off to sleep.

'Mrs Moffat, why don't you rest here?' Judith suggested. 'The sun is warm and you can put your feet up. You work so hard, up at the crack of dawn, and deserve a little respite. I'll take care of Lady Antonia.'

It worked like a charm, Mrs Moffat agreeing readily. Judith and Antonia went off to find Tom. He was waiting impatiently, taking off his hat and beaming at Judith while flushing to the roots of his hair. 'My lady, I've been waiting…' he stammered, and Antonia prodded her in the back so that she stepped closer to him.

'Well done,' she ventured, having no idea what to say. 'I'm so pleased that I can rely on you. Tell me, how far would you go to show your devotion?' She had rehearsed this little speech with Antonia.

To her astonishment he dropped to his knees before her, face uplifted, a beam of sunlight striking across his handsome features. 'I'd do anything… fight dragons… face the fiercest foe!' he exclaimed.

'Get up, Tom. Don't be foolish.' She was flustered, fighting the impulse to draw him close and feel his arms enfolding her.

He stood looking downcast. 'I'm sorry, my lady. I was too bold, but not disrespectful, I promise you. I meant every word.'

'I'm sure you did,' Antonia butted in, though she had been apparently absorbed in petting Sultan. 'It is comforting to know you would help Lady Judith if she asked you.' She returned to petting her stallion.

Judith remembered her instructions, and it came naturally to her to stand close to Tom, reach out and clasp his hand, feel him tremble and edge closer until he slid an arm round her waist.

This decided the matter. She had never before been held by a man of her own age. The only male embraces she had known were Steven's. It was exciting to be pressed close to Tom's chest, to hear his quickened breathing and feel his hands moving up her back and shoulders. She wanted more, and lifted her face to receive his kiss. It was a lovely moment in her life and he seemed skilled in kissing, no doubt practicing on the maidservants and village girls. But that was all he did, simply kissed her lips and then withdrew a little.

'You're my lord's wife,' he muttered. 'This doesn't seem right. I shall be in deep trouble if it is found out.'

'It won't be, I can assure you,' Judith answered, her hands clasped in his. 'In fact I have a proposition to put to you.' She took a deep breath. 'I am unhappily married and want to leave this place. Would you help to organise my escape, and that of Lady Antonia?'

'Could I come with you?' His boyish enthusiasm was infectious.

'Of course.' She gripped his hands tightly and felt the returning pressure.

53

'And dare I hope that you would look upon me as your swain? I know it is a great deal to ask, you being a lady and me a groom, but I feel that we share something.'

'Let us see what the future holds. If we run away then we can join Lady Antonia's troop.'

'They are waiting for me in a derelict farmhouse on the moor,' Antonia chipped in. 'Fell Farm. Do you know it? Can you take us there?'

'I can find it, my lady. Yes, I'll do whatever you say.' Judith, not only following Antonia's instructions but because she longed to be in his arms again, let him lead her to a heap of straw in a secluded corner, while Antonia kept watch.

There his diffidence vanished and Judith enjoyed the lovemaking of a young man, his caresses and kisses bringing her to a state of frenzy when she almost, but not quite, yielded her body to him. As it was Antonia's instructions rang in her ears and she held off from the final surrender, but employed her hands to fondle his engorged member. She was aroused by this action, having always avoided touching Steven's. She was fascinated by this appendage, which throbbed in her grasp and, finally, gave up its emission.

'Oh, my lady… sweetest of women!' he gasped, wiping her hand on his shirttail. 'Thank you! And there will be more?'

Judith sat up and adjusted her clothing, throbbing with the need for fulfilment but following Antonia's advice. She must keep him hanging on until the escape was complete, then, and only then, would she allow herself the enjoyment of having him possess her. It would be worth all the danger and difficulties.

Mrs Moffat was stirring and it was time to leave.

Antonia and Judith walked back to the house talking of light matters, and it was not until evening that they were alone and able to lay their plans.

Chapter 3

Next morning Judith was awakened early by Steven leaping from bed and rushing downstairs. She got up and went to the window, to see him on the front steps in his nightshirt, in eager discussion with a travel-stained man on a horse, who was gabbling excitedly. They went inside and shortly after Steven reappeared and flung on his clothes.

'What has happened?' she dared to ask.

'We are ordered to aid some of our fellows who have a Royalist house under siege in the next county. They are proving stubborn and more soldiers are needed. I'll gather my men together and leave at once. You will be in charge here, along with Mrs Moffat and Mr Barnes. See to it that all runs smoothly in my absence.'

Judith's heart was banging in her chest. Her prayers had been answered. He was going away. Give it a day or two and her plans could be put into operation. Still, she had to appear concerned. 'Oh, husband! Be careful! I will guard Ferris Mead until your return.'

I'm turning into an accomplished liar, she thought, while she dressed and helped him to prepare. By now the village men were used to suddenly leaving their fields and crops in the care of their womenfolk and marching off with their lord and master. It had become a way of life for them. Judith was aware of a sense of anticipation as they transformed themselves from farmers into fighting men. Some, of course, would never return to their wives and children, but this was a risk they were prepared to take.

After what seemed hours Judith waved him off, relief foremost in her mind. It was wicked to pray that he would not come back, but she had gone beyond believing what the preachers had expounded, that those with evil thoughts went to hell. All she was concerned about was enjoying the here and now, and she controlled the urge to run up the stairs and tell Antonia what had transpired. Instead she took her time and eventually arrived as a maid was removing the breakfast dishes.

'What's all the fuss about?' Antonia asked.

The bubble of excitement within Judith was hard to contain. 'He's gone, with his men to help siege a Royalist stronghold. It is heaven sent, surely? He'll be away for a while and this will make it easier for us to leave. Give it a couple of days and we can make our escape in the early hours of the morning, just as it is getting light.'

Antonia turned to her with shining eyes. 'Can you smuggle in my clothes?'

'Yes, and your sword. Should I wear a male outfit?'

'I think not. The three of us will appear to be a man and his wife and a servant, played by Tom. We'll talk to him about it today.'

'It will be easier now Steven has gone. Mrs Moffat will grow slack, so will Mr Barnes. Both like to rob the wine cellar during his absence. They are clever in their juggling with the bottles. He never notices. When we decide to make a run for it I'll lace their drinks with a sleeping draught I make from herbs.'

Judith surprised herself with her own cunning.

She behaved circumspectly, locking the door of Antonia's room behind her and making sure that the staff were going about their duties. As usual Mrs Moffat accompanied them on their afternoon walk, but Judith noticed that her attention was not on her task of duenna, as if her mind was occupied with something else, probably the contents of the wine cellar. When she settled down on the bench outside the stable Judith noticed that she took a small flask from under her shirts, waiting rather impatiently for them to disappear inside.

'I told you,' she whispered to Antonia. 'She likes her tipple.'

'This will make it so much easier for us.'

Judith slipped into Tom's arms in the dimness, and she and Antonia told him of their plans. He was the only groom left. The others had gone off to fight.

'Can we trust you?' Judith sat on a hay bale, her fingers entwined with his.

'I swear it!' he exclaimed, offended that she should doubt him. 'Tell me when and I'll have Sultan harnessed and two others, one for you and one for me. Don't worry, I know my way around these parts even after dark, and can guide you safely to Fell Farm.'

'You'll be an outcast from friends and family,' Antonia warned.

'I don't care,' he declared stoutly. 'What is there here for me? I want adventure!'

'I can promise you that, if little else. You can become a member of my troop and be trained in the use of sword and pistol. You too, Judith.' She had become stern and it was easy to imagine her in command when it came to action. 'We'll arrange this for two nights from now. Do you both agree?'

'Yes,' they answered in unison, and Judith kissed and caressed him, but though wanting to go further, Mrs Moffat was waking and it was time to leave.

That evening, freed from Steven's demanding presence, Judith lingered with Antonia after fixing her bandage. The staff were slack and Mrs Moffat and Mr Barnes nowhere in evidence, probably in the cellar.

'Stay awhile,' Antonia urged and opened her arms wide. 'Let us do what we've had the urge to do ever since we met.' She held her close and kissed her, long and deep. Her tongue probed between Judith's lips and the sensation was heavenly, every nerve in her body responding. It was as good as when Tom had done it, maybe even better for he was a raw lad, nothing like as experienced.

Judith released herself for a moment, saying, 'I'll lock the door.' When she turned back it was to find Antonia already on the bed, beckoning to her. Now she felt nervous, aware that life would never be the same after this. She sank down beside Antonia, who leaned over her, gently kissing her face, neck and ears, then unfastening her bodice and slipping it down to the waist. Her own was already undone, revealing her firm breasts.

'Touch me,' she murmured and, greatly daring, Judith cupped them and let her thumbs revolve on the nipples. It was a heady sensation and her own tingled in unison, just as they had done when Tom caressed them. Antonia let her head rest back against the pillows, eyes closed.

'Am I doing this well?' Judith wanted so much to please this woman who had become her friend.

In answer Antonia raised her skirt, revealing her shapely thighs and the dark wedge of her pubis. Judith thought of that first night when she had secretly watched her rubbing herself, and could not resist reaching over and touching her there. The curling hair was warm, and, 'Go on,' Antonia insisted. 'Do to me what you perform on yourself, and then I'll return the pleasure, I promise.'

Judith felt the lips swell and part beneath her fingers, and remembering how her own body reacted used the same method to bring about Antonia's climax. Her own longing rose within her as she spread the dampness up her partner's sex and onto her nubbin, her excitement increasing as Antonia began to moan and arch her pelvis to meet that provocative touch. Although Judith wanted to delay and learn more about this feminine form of loving Antonia was already in a state of bliss, gasping as she reached her peak.

'Oh, yes! Yes!' she cried, and then slumped, sighing her contentment, smiling up at Judith. 'Is this the first time you've pleasured a woman?'

'Yes.'

'Did you enjoy it?' Antonia reached across and slid a hand under Judith's skirt.

'I did. And I liked bringing Tom off, too.'

Antonia gave a throaty chuckle. 'So you will enjoy the best of both worlds, sweetheart. Now it is my turn to give you the ultimate joy.'

With one hand she toyed with Judith's nipples, while the other opened her cleft and massaged her throbbing bud. She wanted it to last forever, but the feeling rose and rose, finally swamping her. She tried to restrain her groans, fearful that someone might hear, but it was useless, the sensation too fierce and overwhelming.

They lay in one another's arms, and Judith had never known such peace. She felt complete at last, realising that sexual congress could be an expression of affection, and there was nothing unclean about it.

'We will escape the day after tomorrow,' Antonia said. 'Your new life will be hazardous, but there's so much for you to learn. You're going to be free, dear heart.'

It was still dark, but the sky was lightening in the east and a solitary bird started to twitter. Judith stood in the stable, lit by a shaded lantern. The horses were ready, and Tom bent and cupped his hands so that she might step into them and be raised to sit side-saddle. Antonia was already mounted, clad in dark clothing, her buff coat fastened with her valise on the back of Sultan. It was too conspicuous, a warlike garment, and she wanted to appear as a civilian, though she wore her sword, as did all gentlemen of station.

'Ready?' asked Tom, opening the stable doors, extinguishing the lamp and leading his own mount outside.

'Ready,' they chorused.

Judith was terrified that someone would hear the sound of hooves, but the house remained in darkness and there were no shouts of alarm. Tom used a path leading to the back and from there into a narrow lane. Judith followed and it became easier as dawn approached. Then he came out into the open and started to trot, faster and faster, breaking into a gallop. It was exhilarating. Judith couldn't believe it had been so easy.

They covered the miles to Fell Farm without mishap. Because it was Sunday the shepherds and field workers were absent, preparing for church. The moor stretched ahead and Tom led them across it, his knowledge of the area invaluable. It was almost too easy and Judith was afraid that something might go wrong.

'There it is,' he shouted, pointing with his whip to where a house lay in a hollow, and even as he spoke two soldiers hefting muskets reared up from behind a bush.

'Halt!'

They reined in and Antonia raised her hand. 'It's all right. I'm Captain Durward.' She pulled off her hat. 'Don't you remember me? These are my companions, who have helped me to escape.'

At once their attitude changed. They threw down their weapons and ran to Antonia, seizing her hands and acclaiming, 'Thank God! We couldn't have delayed much longer. We're running out of provisions.' It was then that Judith realised they were women too.

She dismounted, following Tom and Antonia as they led their sweating mounts into the yard of the derelict farm. More soldiers came out to greet them and one was in the forefront, flinging her arms round Antonia. 'You're safe! Thank God!'

'We'll leave for Oxford at once, Frankie. You've done well, keeping the others together and waiting for me.' She turned to Judith and introduced her. 'This is Judith Ashley, the wife of my captor, who helped me escape. She is joining us and so is Tom Maslin, without whose aid we should never have got away. Judith, Tom, meet my second-in-command, Frankie Mackinnon, a mercenary soldier who decided to link up with us. I left her in charge when I was captured.'

It was almost too much to take in – the soldiers, male and female, the farmhouse where the roof had collapsed and only the large kitchen was habitable. They seized the loaves and cheese she had brought with her, sharing it as best they could, falling upon it ravenously. Then they made ready to leave, concealing their weapons and pretending to be pilgrims on their way to a religious gathering. Antonia had no intention of getting involved in another skirmish on their journey to Oxford.

Isobel flirted her fan, already bored although the ball had only just begun. Men were thin on the ground, for the summer offensive was in full swing and they had been called away to fight. There were disturbing rumours about battles won by the Roundheads under the leadership of Cromwell.

She wondered what would happen should the Royalists suffer defeat. Normally she dismissed unpleasant thoughts, but this was becoming pressing. She owned a mansion in Paris and had deposited some of her money in a bank there, but had the rest with her and still received the proceeds from her estate, but should her property be taken by the enemy she would be in difficulties.

That night the presence of King Charles and his French queen, Henrietta Maria, were reassuring, but these two diminutive regal people were like something from another age, seeming to brush off any suggestion that their forces might be beaten and themselves captured. He, in particular, was convinced that God had appointed him to rule England, and though a Protestant, was completely under the domination of his vivacious Roman Catholic wife.

Isobel revered them, but listened to the gossip and

pondered on why the king preferred the advice of sycophantic courtiers rather than that of Prince Rupert, his military-minded and experienced nephew. They were a decorous couple, and there were never any rumours regarding royal mistresses or debauchery. He was scholarly and serious-minded, and they were devoted to one another and their children.

The splendid candlelit room reserved for this entertainment was a part of the university that had become the Court ever since the royals arrived there at the start of the war. Isobel knew many of the people who had followed their monarch from London, but was worried about Antonia, for reports maintained she had been captured by the opposing side. Communication was difficult but she gathered that she was being held hostage. She fretted, but there was nothing she could do, except hope.

Rather than stay at home brooding she had accepted this invitation, and wore a new gown made by a French dressmaker who was established in Oxford. The fashion that year among the well-off was for pastel shades. Her skirt was of green silk, very full and worn over a rustling petticoat, the waist slightly higher than normal, the bodice square cut and low, the sleeves full to the elbow where they were gathered in and finished with a lace frill.

Her hairdresser had coaxed her locks into ringlets over each ear, added a wispy fringe on her brow, and swept the rest into a coronet at the crown of her head. She wore pearls around her neck and in her ears. Her cheeks were rouged, as were her lips, and her face powered.

It was a sedate gathering and the string orchestra were playing a pavane. Some were dancing to this stately measure, while the king and queen occupied throne-like chairs on a dais, though Henrietta's feet were tapping as if she would like to join in. Isobel eyed the men, wondering if one of them would want her as his partner, though she would have preferred something livelier.

She wanted to escape and go home, but protocol demanded that no one left until the royal pair had retired. Working her way to the back of the room she stood against the wall near an arras. Everyone near her were watching the dancers and talking, and she was astonished when a hand suddenly appeared from behind the tapestry curtain and yanked her into the small anti-room behind it.

'Got you!' whispered Jamie Westbury, grinning down at her, his face barely illumined by the single candle on the table behind him.

'What do you think you're doing?' she demanded, though unable to help returning his smile.

'I'm about to fuck you, fair lady,' and he bent to kiss her.

He was good-looking, elegant in dark-blue velvet, with a wide white collar and cuffs; just what she needed at that time, the soirée boring in the extreme. He was already raising her skirts and finding his way to her crotch. His mouth was enflaming her, using enough force to wind his tongue with hers. But *here*, within a stone's throw of their monarch? This was too much, even for her.

'Stop it, Jamie,' she murmured, although his fingers were causing mayhem in her body. 'Wait until we can leave, and then come back to my house.'

'I don't think I *can* wait,' he protested, guiding her hand down to his erection. 'I shall spend in my breeches at any moment.'

She gave his penis a hard squeeze. 'Keep it until later.'

'But I want you now.' He inserted a finger into her low neckline, landing on a nipple. She gasped and wriggled free. It was tempting to perform the act right there in the midst of that pompous crowd, but even she didn't have the nerve. Just supposing they were discovered. She would probably be banished from Court. Though many were aware of her lifestyle, some disapproving, others uncaring, such an indiscretion would ruin her reputation.

'Oh, Jamie,' she moaned. 'And I want you too, but let us join in the dancing and get away when we are able. It will soon be over. The king and queen never stay up late. Be patient and control that rampant beast of yours.'

They slipped through the arras and made their way to the floor. Isobel was an accomplished dancer and so was Jamie, but her mind wasn't on it. He guided her through the complicated steps and she was very aware of the touch of his hand, and their closeness some of the time, until they parted, while he bowed and she curtsied. The music ceased and there was a smattering of applause.

He accompanied her as they joined the spectators and she said, 'Is there any word of Antonia?'

'Not yet.' His face became serious. 'I wish I had gone with her but she left me in control here. I've been following her instructions and drilling the rest of them. Don't worry, Isobel. She's very resourceful, and will be back with us before long. I'm sure of it.'

King Charles and Queen Henrietta had risen and, with their attendants, were saying their goodnights. He spoke clearly but with a slight hesitation, thanking them for coming and walking among the crowd who parted to let him and his wife through. The gentlemen bowed low, and the ladies dropped into deep curtsies, but at last it was over and Isobel sent her maidservant to fetch her wrap. Jamie raised her hand to his lips, bending to plant a kiss on the back of it.

'I'll ride in your coach,' he said with a look in his eyes that made her tingle. 'My manservant will bring my horse.'

Every sensible thought was banished from her when she imagined the dark privacy of her carriage and what they would do there. 'My maid can saddle up behind him.'

Within minutes a groom had lowered the step so that she might climb in, followed by Jamie. Hardly had the door closed before he had her in a tight embrace. Speed was of the essence. It was not a great distance to her house and this was to be an aperitif before the main course. He pulled off his hat and unfastened his sword-belt. She lay back in the padded seat and opened her legs. He knelt between them and, regardless of her pleasure, thrust his penis into her, hard and deep, again and again. The coach rattled over the uneven road and Isobel strained upwards, trying to find pressure on her clitoris, but Jamie had ejaculated before she had time to settle into a rhythm that would bring her to orgasm.

Jamie pulled away, occupied the seat opposite her and adjusted his attire, hat in place again, and sword in place at his left hip. Isobel fumbled for her handkerchief and stuffed it between her thighs, soaking up his emission. 'That will do for now,' she said into the darkness, illumined only by a house lamp now and again, or that of a tavern or late opening shop. 'I expect more later.'

'And you shall have it,' he promised earnestly. 'I

was so hot for you that I lost control.'

'Well don't let it happen again,' she warned.

Judith was so tired that she had a hard job keeping awake as her horse covered the miles. She had to remain alert in order to keep up with Tom and Antonia and the rest of them. So this was adventure, was it? Whatever happened it must be better than living with Steven, surely?

They had ridden non-stop, apart from short breaks to relieve nature. Avoiding villages and using byways they were in sight of Oxford and it was getting dark again. Antonia led them to the main gate where they were stopped by guards, but welcomed in when they recognised her. They clattered through the town, once a peaceful seat of learning but now taken over by the military, the king's supporters, and the hustle and bustle of war.

Judith could do nothing but follow Antonia along streets lit by flares, past shops, buildings, inns and eating establishments, until they arrived at a pair of imposing gates, which at her command were opened by the lodge-house keeper.

'Welcome to my home,' Antonia shouted and there, beyond a short drive, stood an imposing house where lights twinkled in the windows.

The twenty-odd troopers dismounted and took their horses to the rear to be stabled and fed. Judith could see lights beyond this area, and glimpsed tents with people moving in and out of them. Antonia came to stand beside her and Tom, explaining, 'The house is big, but some of my followers camp in the garden when we're not called out. Come inside, you need food and a rest.' She swung round to ask a mature man in charge, 'Sergeant Miller, where is Lieutenant

Westbury?'

'His Majesty is holding a soirée. He was invited, and it is not politic to refuse.'

'Ah,' mused Antonia. 'I see, and I suppose Lady Isobel is attending, too?'

'No doubt.' The sergeant gave a knowing smile that Antonia returned. He was one of her most trustworthy men and there was little that happened in and around her platoon that escaped his notice.

Judith was hustled into the house and up the stairs to Antonia's apartment. Tom went with them. They followed her into a lofty room where the wood-panelled walls had been painted white and hung with tapestries. Servants ran ahead to light candles. Antonia's maid came to see if her mistress needed anything. 'No, I'm going out again shortly, but I want you to give Lady Judith a room next to mine and see that she has everything she wants. The gentleman, too. Is this what you want, Judith?'

Tom was smiling widely, although as travel-stained as herself. Judith wanted nothing more than to fall into bed and sleep, but he had served them loyally and she felt it was her duty to reward him. The idea was pleasant, and she was certain that after a rest she would be only too glad to celebrate her freedom in his arms.

When Antonia had assured herself that those who'd ridden with her were being looked after, she selected a fresh horse and rode to Isobel's residence. She knew that the king and queen retired early, and had little doubt that Isobel would be at home by now and, in all probability, escorted by Jamie. She needed to see them, to relax her vigilance and organising powers and take a bath, listen to the latest gossip and

68

idle in Isobel's bed, making love with either or both of them. Judith's inexperience was charming, but now she needed her own kind, those who had tasted sexual diversities.

The front door was opened by a footman. 'Is she here?' Antonia demanded, stepping inside.

'She is, my lady,' he answered.

'Then look to my horse. See that he is stabled.'

With that she took the stairs two at a time and arrived outside Isobel's bedchamber. She knocked loudly. 'Who is it?' Isobel answered impatiently.

'Antonia.'

'Oh, thank God! Come in, come in!'

The room was as luxurious as she remembered, and Isobel occupied her massive four-poster with Jamie at her side. Both were naked. 'Nothing has changed, I see,' Antonia commented, and started to take off her outer garments. 'I need a bath.'

'The tub has not been emptied since I used it earlier, in my dressing-room. The water will be tepid by now but I'll ring for some buckets of hot. Where the devil have you been? I'm glad to see you.' Isobel sat up, smiling widely, and Antonia was touched by her concern.

'You mustn't worry about me. I can take care of myself. I was aided in my escape by the wife of my captor, Lady Judith Ashley, who has run away from him and come to join us. She's lovely. I expect you to take her under your wing. Don't trouble about the contents of the bath; it will be fine as it is. But keep the bed warm for me.'

It was good to strip and immerse herself in the wooden tub filled with scented water. It was chilly, but that didn't bother her. She kept her injured arm as dry as she could, but the bandage soon became wet and she took it off. The wound was healing well and she doubted that she would be scarred much. Soldier she might be, but she were essentially a woman and revelled in perfume, and soap, and all the niceties of being female. Her hair needed washing so she ducked her head under the water, running her fingers through her curls. Although she had enjoyed Judith she was eager to receive the more sophisticated attentions of Isobel and Jamie.

She emerged from the dressing-room wrapped in a towel and Isobel exclaimed, 'Your arm! What have you done?'

'It was a sword slash I received while trying to fight off those who wanted to take me prisoner. Don't worry; Judith has been caring for it. I have a spare bandage in my pocket. Will you fasten it on for me?'

While Isobel was playing nurse Jamie wanted to hear all about the fight and subsequent escape. She recounted her adventures while he towelled her hair and her arm was bandaged. Then Isobel ordered supper and they ate it in bed, washed down with wine.

'What were you doing when I so rudely interrupted?' Antonia asked, toasting them over the rim of her glass.

'Fucking, of course. What else?'

Antonia placed her drink on the nightstand and eased down under the covers. 'Well carry on, and let me watch.'

'You'll not only watch, but join us,' Isobel insisted, whipping the quilt back and exploring Antonia's sleek curves. 'I've missed you, dearest. We must make up for lost time.'

With Jamie on one side of her and Isobel on the other Antonia gave herself up to wanton, uninhibited pleasure. Though sometimes they played rough games that involved paddles, whips and chains, tonight she needed slow, sensual arousal, and they were sensitive to her mood.

Chapter 4

'Are you happy, my lady?' Tom stood before Judith, twirling his hat in front of him, just as he had done when he was her groom.

She smiled. 'I'm too weary to know. Ask me again when I've slept.'

She was being treated well, everyone grateful to her for helping their leader escape. Supper was served in her room, and it seemed that the staff had been given to understand that she and Tom were a couple. Two pails of water, one hot and one cold, had been placed by the washstand, and Judith was glad to rinse her hands and face before sitting down to eat. Tom, too, although he was not as used to washing as her.

'I swim in the river, sometimes,' he explained, after following her example. 'And once a month when I was younger my foster mother would set the tin bath in front of the kitchen fire and we children would be scrubbed, one after the other.'

Judith gave a mental shudder, although she did not bathe often. She had been brought up to believe that baring the body was unseemly, a view also held by Steven. She could hardly credit that she was eating supper in a bedroom with a former servant, and about to sleep with him. She felt awkward when the dishes had been removed and they were alone again. Antonia was not there to guide her and she had to follow her own instincts. Half hidden by the bed curtains she took off her clothing and put on a nightgown, then slipped between the covers. She turned her eyes away as Tom undressed, hung his garments over the back of a chair and donned a clean nightshirt before climbing in beside her.

They lay on their backs, like two stone effigies in a church, and he ventured to take her hand in his. 'Don't worry, my lady. You don't have to do anything. Getting away from my tedious life was reward enough, but I do want to make love to you, though can't believe that you should so honour me.'

Judith couldn't keep her eyes open, the soft, warm mattress beneath and this loving companion at her side making sleep irresistible. 'Dear Tom,' she murmured. 'Never doubt that I want you, but I'm so, so tired.'

Waves of slumber bore her away for hours, and she was awakened by shafts of sunlight piercing the window drapes. For a moment she didn't recall where she was, and then reality brought her sharply to herself. Tom snuggled against her. His nightshirt had ridden up and she could feel his erection pressing against her side. It was so pleasant that she wriggled her hips, letting him know she was aware. His arm clasped her and his lips were on her neck, kissing her skin.

How wonderful it was to find this kindly youth embracing her instead of her cold, selfish husband. Her joy was quickly transmuted into desire, especially when his fingers wandered down to her cleft and sought out her bud, caressing it in a knowing manner. He was aware of what women wanted. The way he carefully roused her, parting her lower lips and concentrating on the swollen clitoris was similar to Antonia's touch.

'Where did you learn to be such a good lover?' Judith whispered, than quickly added, 'No, don't stop. I'm enjoying it so much.'

'I was shown how to do it by the village lasses,' he said with a chuckle. 'I did it to them and then they brought me off by hand, and that way we all enjoyed ourselves and there was no fear of a baby.'

He continued to stroke her until she was overwhelmed with pleasure and came. Then needing his weapon inside her she lay back and urged him to enter her, crooning, 'Ah, ah... yes, yes... that feels so good. Go on, fuck me hard. That's it. Harder, harder.'

She was still contracting from her own climax and needed his large cock inside her, giving her muscles something to clench around. This was the first time such a thing had been possible. Steven had never satisfied her and she hated the feel of his member in her dry vagina. Tom had made her very wet, and she welcomed his possession.

No matter what happens or how far our paths divide I shall never, never forget him, she vowed inwardly, clinging to him with her arms about his neck and her legs clasping his waist so he could penetrate deeper. His face resembled that of a martyred saint as his final spasms shook him. He slumped down, crushing her beneath him, resting his head on her shoulder.

Judith recovered, shifting from under him but keeping her arms around him, not wishing him to feel rejected. 'That was lovely,' she whispered. 'Lord Ashley never satisfied me. This is the very first time I've known the enjoyment of making love with a man.'

He grinned at her. 'Is that so, my lady? I can hardly believe it, him being an educated gentleman and all.'

'That doesn't necessarily make him a good lover. You were far, far better. Let's do it again.' Judith was inspired to try different positions. This was only the start. There would be other men, she was certain, but just for the moment Tom was all she wanted.

Feeling completely refresh and invigorated Antonia left Isobel early, dragging Jamie with her. She needed to know what had been happening during her absence.

'It seems we're losing our hold in many places,' he said gloomily.

'Our armies are spread too thin.' She was eyeing her own force drilling under Sergeant Miller, presenting arms and being put through their paces. He was a hard taskmaster. 'Where is Prince Rupert?'

Jamie shrugged. 'Here, there and everywhere. No wonder the Roundheads call him the Devil Prince because he seems to be in all places at once. But you know His Highness. He thinks nothing of riding for hours with his elite force, through night and storm and all sorts if he thinks he's needed to bolster the courage of a garrison, or add his weight to a beleaguered city.'

Oh yes, Antonia knew the prince, in the biblical sense as well as admiring him for his military achievements. She'd told Judith that it was not wise to lose your heart to a man, and this was from bitter experience. Practically every woman who met Rupert fell in love with him, and she was no exception. He was tall and slim, with curling black hair and dark Stuart eyes inherited from his mother, the king's sister who had married a German prince. Antonia admired him for his knowledge not only of warfare, but languages, drawing, and science. He was abstemious, and didn't waste his time whoring and drinking like some of the other commanders.

She could listen to him talking for hours, his accented voice pleasing her ears, and the tales of his adventures. He was in the army in Europe at thirteen; his mother had so many children that she, an exile, could not afford to keep the boys at home. Rupert was captured and imprisoned in a castle in Austria when he was eighteen, stayed there four years, and was only released on condition that he fought for his uncle in England.

Antonia had met him when he was at low ebb, after arguing with the king's advisers who knew very little about how to manage a campaign. Governor of Bristol, a city he had taken from the enemy, he often rode into Oxford to consult with the king, who he found exasperating. He met up with Antonia and she invited him to review her troops. They had talked far into the night and ended up in bed.

Great soldier he might be, but he was an inexperienced lover. Those years in prison had not helped, away from female company. This was endearing and she found it hard to control her feelings for him, though knowing it was useless. She kept this a secret, confiding in no one, especially him.

'He'll be here soon,' Jamie added. 'Meanwhile, you should address the new recruits.'

Judith and Tom were told to see Antonia. She was in the reception room, seated at a long table with two other men, one old and bearded, one young and personable. Some newcomers stood in line, shuffling their feet awkwardly.

When Antonia saw Judith she left the rest to her officers and rose to meet her. 'Did you sleep well?' she enquired, taking her hand.

'Oh yes. I feel much better.'

'So do I, ma'am,' Tom chipped in.

'You may call me captain whilst I'm dressed like this,' Antonia corrected, indicating her masculine attire. 'Now then, both of you, what role do you see yourselves playing here?'

'I want to learn how to use a sword and handle myself in a battle,' Tom answered promptly. 'And you, Judith?'

'I'd like to do the same,' she said, though now having seen how the soldiers lived, she wasn't so sure.

Antonia's eyes twinkled. 'You find the reality daunting? Sleeping under canvas, cooking over open fires?'

'I'm willing to try.'

'This isn't a game.' Antonia became serious. 'You may be fighting for your life. But if you are sincere then I'll supply you with suitable clothes and you can sleep in one of the tents tonight, and live as the others do. You may find that you'd rather join the women in the baggage wagons, nursing the wounded and bringing comfort to the dying.'

This was something of a shock. Judith had had the vague notion that she would be residing in the house with Antonia.

'I'm ready to try being a soldier,' she answered, though guessing that the training would be short and hard so that, when the call came, they would be ready.

She was given shirts, doublets and breeches, socks,

boots and a hat, and then told to go back to her room and change. Tom was sent off in another direction to begin his transformation into a fighter.

Judith went upstairs and spread the garments on the bed. They seemed to be around her size. It was exhilarating, and she wished Steven was there to see her and be angered. Would she ever meet him again? Maybe in a battle somewhere? She admitted to herself that the thought of actually coming face to face with him made her feel sick.

She stripped to her chemise, donned the shirt, buttoned it and then added the socks. After this she tackled the knee-breeches. When they were fastened the effect was pleasing. The riding boots came next and the woollen doublet, and she found herself transformed into a young man.

'Well done,' said Antonia, coming in at the door. 'You look the part. All the girls will be after you, and many of the men, I suspect. How do you feel?'

'Strange.' Judith examined her image in the mirror. 'But yes, breeches are more comfortable than skirts, especially if one has to move around quickly. It will take some getting used to. Will I make a swordsman, do you think?'

'We shall see when Sergeant Miller tries you out. Come, kiss me, and tell me about your night with Tom.'

Judith could feel her cheeks reddening. Her emotions were confused. Antonia's arms around her were so comforting, it was like coming home. But Tom? Ah, Tom had been something different entirely. 'I slept at first with him beside me, but when I woke at dawn it was to find him hard and ready. I acted from instinct, it seemed, which is what I had always been denied by Steven. I learned about the

77

male organ, had it in me and enjoyed it. He knew how to bring me to pleasure, having practiced with the village girls. It was remarkable.'

Antonia chuckled and hugged her harder. 'I'm so glad. Now you see that it is possible to enjoy men and women. Last night I had both, Jamie Westbury and my dear friend, Isobel. He was already rogering her when I reached her house. All three of us enjoyed one another. I shall introduce you to her, a most remarkable lady, and Jamie, too. That's him over there, Lieutenant Westbury. Then maybe one day soon you will meet Prince Rupert.'

'Is he very handsome?' Judith could feel desire rising again as Antonia caressed her breasts through the shirt.

'Oh, yes. Probably the most handsome man I have ever clapped eyes on.' There was an inflection in Antonia's voice that made Judith stare at her. Then she smiled and kissed her lingeringly on the lips, and added, 'He's a great solider, renowned for his cavalry charges. Now come; I shall hand you over to the sergeant who will put you through your paces. See how you manage, and if it isn't for you then we need help in the wagons.'

Judith held out her purse. It was full of money for she had robbed Steven's strongbox and taken all she could carry. 'Will you look after this for me? It is all I possess. I'll keep a little and come to you when I need more.'

That day was the most arduous of her life. First she moved her few belongings into a large tent shared by several other women, all veterans it seemed. She knew one of them, Frankie Mackinnon, who was in charge, and it was she who introduced Judith to the others, and then took her to begin training in the square at the back of the house. She saw Tom but they had no chance to speak. There was so much to learn, and by the end of the day she was sure she would never become a competent swordsman, aching in every limb.

She used the latrines situated at the back of the field, then ate supper of broth and bread and settled down on the floor of the tent, wrapped in her cloak with her head upon a makeshift pillow, too tired to pay much attention to the others. They were chattering and laughing. Some were going out to meet their lovers, whilst others cuddled up together under the blankets. Tom was quartered a little further off.

After two days of this her muscles ached a little less and she was starting to understand the rules of fencing. 'Well done,' said Frankie, and there was admiration in her eyes. Judith recognised that look, and also the pressure of the arm resting around her shoulders that was more than just comradely. 'Come to the tavern with me tonight and I'll buy you a bumper of ale.'

Judith was curious to find out more about this confident girl, but said, 'I already have another engagement. Captain Durward is taking me to meet a friend of hers, Baroness Thorley.'

'Is she indeed?' Frankie didn't sound too pleased. 'She's highborn, helps the cause and entertains soldiers, both men and women.'

There was something in her tone that indicated more, but it didn't spoil Judith's anticipation of an evening spent in more comfortable surroundings. She was finding it hard to live rough, missing clean linen, well cooked food and a comfortable bed. Sharing the latrines with both sexes was unavoidable and

79

embarrassing, and the washing facilities were provided by a stream.

As instructed she went to Antonia's apartment and there bathed and changed into female clothing, delighted to find that a gown had been selected for her, finer than anything she had ever worn. Beth helped both her and her mistress to get ready, a cheerful woman who had attended Antonia for years.

'It's rather like the old days, my lady, before this wretched war,' she remarked, pinning up Antonia's hair and threading it with pearls.

'Life will never be quite the same again, whatever the outcome,' she replied, slipping easily into the role of a fashionable lady. She turned to Judith. 'You look radiant, and Frankie tells me your swordsmanship is improving. How are you finding camp life?'

'Uncomfortable but interesting,' she answered truthfully, hardly able to believe that the beauty looking back at her from the pier-glass was herself.

Antonia appeared beside her. 'I'm proud of you. Sergeant Miller tells me you're quick to learn and have a natural agility. Brave too, and able to seize any advantage. Frankie speaks highly of you. I think she finds you desirable, but watch her, for she falls in and out of love easily.'

Judith changed the subject. 'Tom is doing well. He's practicing with the pike. There's no shortage of women fancying him. He'll soon get over me, though we'll still be friends.'

Antonia gave a twirl, admiring her refection. 'Of course you will, but never forget that the danger is real. This isn't a game. Be prepared to lose friends.'

With this warning ringing in her ears Judith accompanied her downstairs, through the hall and out of the main door to where a carriage awaited them. It was almost as if the war didn't exist. A coachman in livery sat on his box out front, flicking his long whip, and grooms leapt down from the back to help the ladies enter the interior.

'I didn't expect...'Judith began, settling down on the upholstered seat.

'To find this? Did you think we'd be walking to Isobel's? When I'm on leave I like to enjoy the comforts of life. Don't worry; the horses are borrowed from the cavalry for the evening. They're much sought after by both sides, needed in battle for pulling artillery and the wagons. And if food runs short and the soldiers can't purloin cattle or chickens on the march, then they sometimes have to eat horsemeat.'

Judith took this in. She was learning something new every hour. She wished Steven had discussed such matters with her, but he'd considered her unintelligent, only fit to be a housewife. She had grown up since meeting Antonia.

When she walked into Isobel's reception room it was as if she was taking part in a fairytale. The wealth of candles blazing in wall sconces and overhead, the music played on the spinet, the talk and laughter and, above all, the elegance of the other guests, almost convinced her that the war didn't exist. The gentlemen flaunted love-locks that fell to below their shoulders from under broad-brimmed, plumed hats, and swaggered about in velvet doublets and breeches, the light flashing on their sword hilts. Riding boots with turned-down tops were popular, a reminder that they were probably members of the cavalry.

The ladies equalled their escorts in finery, bold and flirtatious. Judith sensed a kind of desperation in their

81

determination to squeeze every drop of pleasure from the occasion. This way they could blot out the memory of those lost; fathers, husbands, brothers and sons, and of estates taken by the enemy and fortunes diminished.

Antonia led her forward. They approached a woman with auburn curls and face paint, a lovely creature whose bosom was exposed to the nipples by her low bodice. 'Antonia, sweeting!' she chorused, kissing her lips.

'This is Judith. I've told you how she helped me escape.'

'Oh, so brave! You must be rewarded.' Isobel snatched a glass from the tray of a passing footman. 'Drink, my dear, and let me show you the delights I can offer you. Who do you fancy? A lovely woman or a virile, handsome brute of a man?'

Judith was abashed by Isobel's frankness. 'I-I don't know,' she stammered.

'Oh, but you must have someone. I insist. Take your time; watch what the others do and this may inspire you with a wish to join them.'

The wine was red, sweet and heavy with a lingering aftertaste. 'That's right, drink and forget all you ever learned in your Puritan upbringing,' Antonia advised, and led her by the hand, presenting her to this lady or that gentleman.

Judith began to discover that this was no ordinary gathering. Couples were disporting themselves without reserve, sometimes more than two together. They were blatantly kissing and caressing, finding alcoves or nooks where they could indulge their lust. Judith's single glass of wine made her feel dizzy and wanton, and if these highborn people pandered to their desires, then why not her?

The party became noisier. Maidservants had been instructed to raise their skirts at the back, displaying their buttocks, willing to be fingered by anyone who chose. The footmen stood unmoving, ordered to permit hands of either sex to explore their genitals. Then several haughty women stalked in, naked except for stockings and garters and high-heeled shoes. They flourished whips, driving hard bargains with those who wanted to be dominated.

This was enough to astonish Judith, but there were other sights. One person, who she had thought to be a tall, finely dressed woman, leaned over the back of a chair and whipped up her skirts and petticoats and displayed a man's sexual parts. A gentleman grabbed him round the waist and plunged a large phallus into his rectum. This shocked Judith. She had heard of sodomy, but never before understood its meaning. The spinet tinkled, couples danced and drank and became more outrageous in their behaviour.

'Not yet found a partner?' Isobel's bodice was down around her waist and her breasts were being fondled by raffish Cavalier. 'I'll take you to my sanctum. Come with me.'

She took her through a pair of heavy brocaded curtains into another large room. Judith blinked, wondering about its unusual furnishing. It was lit by candles in floor-standing girandoles, and these shone on strange contraptions; a vaulting horse, chairs without seats, cross-posts, and racks holding canes and birches and manacles. It was like a torture chamber, and yet the occupants were not groaning in pain, but with pleasure.

What remained of the Puritan within her was shocked and embarrassed by the sights that now filled her vision, but the deep, dark core of her was aroused. There was a nude woman chained to the whipping post, arms stretched upwards, face pressed against the wood while a man dressed entirely in black was flogging her, marking her skin with red weals while she cried out and begged him, 'Take me, master! Take me!'

He threw aside the flogger, opened his breeches and thrust between her legs, tied in a wide-spread position. Those watching this entertainment cheered, and continued with their own pleasures. Another girl was tethered to one of the chairs, her genitals exposed through the gap where the seat should have been. Men were fondling her breasts, while another had his cock in her mouth. Meanwhile a man and a woman were under the chair, caressing her private parts through the hole.

A youth was facedown over the vaulting horse, while another man leaned over him, fondling his naked spine and the divide of his buttocks, then spitting on his hand, applying it to his phallus and entering the other's anus. Judith looked away and met Isobel's amused eyes.

'Well, is there anything here that rouses your curiosity to try it?' she asked, her magnificent breasts gleaming in the candlelight.

'No. It's all so new to me. I never dreamed that such scenes could take place. I need time to understand it, your ladyship.'

'Isobel, please.' Her hostess gathered her into her arms. 'I hope this hasn't upset you. There's no hurry. Meanwhile I shall introduce you to a man who is also on his first visit here.' She hailed someone who was leaning against a pillar with his feet crossed at the ankles and his arms folded over his chest. 'Mark,' she called. 'Mark Granger. There's someone I want you to meet.'

He looked at her and straightened, then made his way across. He was of above medium height and well-dressed without being showy, and Judith, though shamed to meet him in such surroundings, was impressed. They were introduced and he offered her his arm. 'Would you like to stroll in the garden?' he asked, and she felt no threat from him.

'Yes,' she said, relieved to get away from the house.

'I shall see you later, my children,' Isobel carolled. 'Enjoy yourselves.'

There were so many new things happening to Judith that she hardly knew which way to turn. Walking out into the garden with a stranger was unheard of, and at night, too!

The moon was bright and the air balmy, and they were not the only ones there. Shadowy figures moved between trees and behind bushes. There were low voices and laughter. Mark paused at a balustrade that bordered a terrace overlooking the lawn.

'Isobel was rather forward in suggesting that we stroll together,' he said, smiling down at Judith in the light of a flare. 'This is her way and I'm certain she meant no harm, but I can take you to join your friends if you prefer. I'm sure you didn't come alone.'

'I'm with Antonia Durward.'

He chuckled. 'Ah, I see. You mean *Captain* Durward.'

'I have joined her troopers.' Judith felt proud of making this admission. She lifted her chin and straightened her spine. 'She was my husband's prisoner and I helped her escape.'

Mark sat on the stone wall. 'Would you care to tell

85

me about it?'

His kindly smile and frank, open countenance encouraged Judith. She felt easy with him, and was aware of a spark between them. Unlike the other men at the gathering he was not trying to take advantage of her in any way. He was one of the nicest people she had met since being in Oxford and she found him easy to talk with, telling her story without hesitation.

'You're a brave lady,' he commented, when she had finished. 'And now you are joining Antonia's soldiers.'

'Do you approve of women in breeches?' she teased him gently, watching his reaction.

He laughed and stood closer to her. 'Women are wonderful whatever they wear. I'm a great admirer of the fair sex, but not, I hasten to assure you, in the same way as those fellows in there,' and he jerked his head towards the scenes taking place in the reception room. 'One day, when all this is over, I hope to settle down with a loving partner and be with her until we both leave this earth.'

His sincerity moved her. She had begun to believe that this was a quality she would never find in a man. 'So you are not yet married?' she ventured, and his hand brushed hers as they leaned on the balustrade.

'I was touring Europe completing my education when the war started and I hurried home to support King Charles. My father is the Earl of Marshfield in the West Country. I left my home and joined Prince Rupert's cavalry. We never settle in one place for long. He is in demand everywhere.'

'Then why are you here at this moment?' Judith was finding him more and more attractive. He was unmarried and personable, taking events as they happened without making a drama of them. A calm,

86

sensible person; and she wanted to know more about him. He didn't have the swaggering bravura of a Cavalier, nor yet the dull, sober sidedness of a Roundhead.

'Rupert is even now in conference with the king. We rode from Bristol today. He has a house here, loaned by a supporter. I know Isobel and she invited me to take time off and enjoy myself, and the best thing that has happened to me tonight is meeting you.'

She drew in a breath, her heart suddenly light. He had some of the qualities of Tom, but there seemed to be a bond between them, as if they had known each other forever. Was he the one she had been seeking all her life? He stepped closer and she could smell him, a clean smell not over-perfumed like some of the dandies, nor yet reeking of sweat. Then without warning she was in his arms while he covered her face with kisses, his hands moving over her silk-covered spine and closing around her waist. Strong hands with nothing lecherous about them, just a loving touch, respectful yet desirous.

'Oh, Judith,' he murmured against her lips. 'This is so sudden, so strange. I don't want you to think me the kind of fellow who takes advantage of a young lady. In all truth I can say that I have never felt like this about a woman before. I won't pretend to be a saint, and have had my lustful moments, but this is the first time it has meant more to me than that.'

His words moved her so much that she tightened her arms around his neck, and he held her closer, hands clasped around her hips. Against her breasts rising above her brief bodice she could feel the embroidery on his doublet and, below that, the hard line of his phallus. Before meeting Antonia she would have struggled away, alarmed by his action, but now she welcomed it.

He eased her against the wall, his arms trapping her on either side while she looked up into his shadowed face. 'I'm still married,' she reminded, while her body responded to his strength.

'I know,' he murmured. 'But your husband is a traitor. You could have the marriage annulled. Do you love him?'

She shook her head. 'No, I have never loved him, nor even respected him. It was a match arranged by my parents when I was fifteen. He was a widower and far older than me.'

'Poor girl. That was cruel. Have you any children?'

'No, and he blamed me for this, although his former wife had none either. I think the fault may have lain with him. When he took Antonia prisoner it was like a revelation. She talked to me, told me that his treatment was wrong, and encouraged me to run off with her.'

'I'm so happy you did.' He bent and kissed her again. Their tongues met and the feel of his hand circling her breast was exciting. He pushed aside the lace to reach her nipple. She moaned her pleasure and pressed up against him.

His breathing quickened and the pressure of his mouth on hers became harder. He pushed his hips against hers with fierce movements and she didn't want him to stop. But he suddenly pulled away from her. He was shaking and he held her at arm's length, his fingers digging into her shoulders.

'What is wrong?' She was terribly afraid that she had offended him somehow.

'You deserve more than this. I won't take you like a common strumpet. I honour you too much for that.

Come back to my lodgings and there we can talk and become better acquainted before we make love. For this is what it will be, I promise you… making love in the true sense of the word. We will find Antonia and tell her where I have taken you. Do you agree?'

The ardour in his eyes and voice convinced her that he was sincere. 'What can I do but accept your invitation?' she whispered. 'Yes, Mark, I will come with you.'

Chapter 5

Steven strode into the house in the blackest rage of his life. Mrs Moffat and Mr Barnes trembled before him, and the other servants stood in a terrified row.

'What has been taking place here?' he bellowed. 'I return with my men this evening to find that all hell has been let loose during my absence.'

'Oh, sir, it was no fault of anyone save her ladyship. We had no notion of what they were planning, she and that unnatural creature who dressed like a man.' Mrs Moffat was wringing her hands together and almost grovelling before him.

'I ordered you to guard her,' he shouted, raising his crop as if he would strike her.

'I did, my lord… indeed I did, but one morning I woke to find they had ridden off and taken one of the grooms with them, young Tom Maslin, sir. I've never known such wickedness.'

'She stole horses?'

'Yes, sir.'

'And what else?'

'Clothes, sir, and food.'

And my money, he thought on an upsurge of fury. I must check my strongbox at once. Meanwhile there was this unreliable pack of idiots to deal with. He turned on his heel, his face set as he fought for control. There was no way he must show weakness in front of them.

'Very well. I want the prisoner's room searched for any clue as to where they went. I need to know if they were seen and what direction they were taking, though I guess it was towards Oxford. If she has joined that Great Malignant, Charles I, then she is no longer my wife and I forbid any of you to utter her name again. Is this understood?'

Thoroughly cowed they hung their heads and nodded. He would have liked to dismiss every one of them, but this would have left him short-staffed and there were more urgent matters to hand. With candle bearers running ahead he stalked up to the chamber he had once shared with Judith, and his anger increased. He wanted to strangle her with his bare hands, his manhood affronted, his name smirched while she ran away with a she-soldier and was probably planning to be one herself, fighting for the Royalists.

Dismissing the servants he went directly to the strongbox kept hidden in the depths of a cupboard. Only he and Judith knew its whereabouts, and she also had access to the key. He'd been reluctant to share this with her, but it had become necessary when he was away so that the running of the establishment could be maintained. He opened the hiding place, holding a candle high. The lid of the iron box was open, and most of the coins were gone. Judith had not only taken his honour, but his money too. No matter that he had another cache of which she knew nothing. The fact that she dared rob him was enough to add fuel to his fire.

Throwing off his buff coat, breastplate and sword, he paced up and down, brooding on what his neighbours would think when news of her behaviour got out. He would be the laughing-stock of the village. Fortunately the conflict was increasing and would take him away a great deal. The fortunes of the Roundheads were on the ascendant.

His whip slashed, striking thin air, but he imagined that Judith was under it, receiving punishment. As he beat her imaginary form again and again so his sexual appetite, repressed while he'd been away, suddenly rose to full strength. He ripped open his breeches and released his cock, rubbing it as he visualised seeing her bleed and cringe. He fed his imagination, giving full rein to the secrets within his mind. Young servant girls forced to yield to him, on their knees, sucking his organ, or maybe the innkeeper's wife, bending over while he thrust into her rectum. Fine ladies taken prisoner by him, chained to rings in the walls while he whipped and fucked them.

He blamed Judith for these thoughts, shouting inwardly, 'You filthy bitch! How dare you take my money and run from me? How dare you play with your genitals, and those of that traitorous whore! You are mine! My wife, my chattel! You should be here to bring me ease. Now I am forced to do it myself, committing a mortal sin!'

He came with sudden force, his emission jetting out. Groaning he clasped himself, then continued to mutter, 'Bitch! Harlot! Whore! Just wait until I catch you, then you'll wish you'd never been born!'

'Look after her, and make sure she reaches my house safely,' Antonia admonished Mark, when they found her at last in the arms of Jamie.

'Don't worry, captain. It would be more than my life's worth if harm came to her.'

'You're not jesting. It certainly would, and you, Judith, take care. Curfew is at midnight and Sergeant Miller will be taking role-call.'

It was a dry evening and Judith and Mark walked the short distance to the tavern where he lodged. 'It's not far from the house loaned to His Highness,' he said. 'I need to be within reach, should there be an emergency.'

Light streamed from the latticed windows and there was the hum of genial voices and sudden bursts of raucous laughter. The door was open wide and Mark conducted her into the public bar. He was greeted at once by some of his comrades and, after introducing her and rousing their interest by saying she was training to be a soldier, he excused himself and conducted her to a private room at the rear. She couldn't avoid hearing the cat-calls, whistles and pieces of bawdy advice that trailed after them.

'I apologise for my friends,' he remarked as he took her cloak. 'I'm afraid the army makes us somewhat coarse in our language.'

'I'm beginning to learn this, even among the females.' Judith sat down after he pulled out a chair for her.

The landlord came in, carrying a bottle of wine and two glasses. He and Mark exchanged pleasantries and he left them. There was silence for a moment, and then Mark poured the wine and made a toast. 'Here's health unto His Majesty.'

She repeated the words and took a sip, then said, 'I

still can't believe I'm here, in Oxford, within a stone's throw of the king. Two weeks ago I was as much a prisoner in my husband's house as Antonia. I never realised how much life there was outside of Ferris Mead.'

'It can be overwhelming. I know so many fellows who have let it go to their heads. Some of them were students in this very university town before suddenly joining the ranks and turning into swaggering, hard-drinking, womanising bullies. Don't let the grim reality of war deaden your sensitivity. You are too fine for that.'

Judith wanted to cry; the stresses, strains and sheer unfamiliarity of the past days sweeping over her. 'I'm not fine at all. I'm a woman who has thrown aside her life and set out on a course unknown to her. I wonder if I have enough courage to carry on. I'm frightened, Mark.'

He was on his knees at her side in an instant, his arms around her. She fumbled for her handkerchief and buried her head in his shoulder. 'Trust me, darling,' he murmured. 'And trust Antonia.'

'But it is useless,' she sobbed. 'You and I will be parted, you to obey Prince Rupert and I to go with her.'

'Have faith. We've found each other and Fate will insure that this bond is not broken. Come upstairs and share my bed for an hour. Then I will order a link-boy and light you back to your quarters by midnight.'

She took his face between her hands and looked into his eyes. 'Are you sincere? Or simply looking for a woman to roger?'

He stared back at her without blinking. 'Trust me. If you prefer we can simply lie in each other's arms like brother and sister, taking comfort from this and harming no one.'

Still doubtful, recalling the scenes at Isobel's orgy, she followed him into the passage and up the winding stairs to his room. It was sparsely furnished but neat, and he dismissed his manservant who, she gathered, travelled everywhere with him. He had told her that he paid for almost everything himself, using the money from his inheritance, a lord but without an estate worth speaking of, decimated by the enemy. What would become of him if he survived was a question to which he had no answer, particularly if the worst happened and the Parliamentarians won.

He went to the table, spread out a sheet of paper and dipped a quill pen into the inkstand. 'I'm giving you my name and title, and instructions as to where you can send messages, though it is doubtful that they will reach me. Will you do the same?'

While she was writing he stretched on the tester bed and then patted the space beside him. Judith went across hesitantly, the unfamiliar room and the man whom she hardly knew tending to dampen her desire. Yet when he folded her in his arms it felt right, as it had done the first time she embraced Antonia. It was even better, for now she had experience of the male, thanks to Tom, and was aware of her own needs.

Everything about Mark appealed to her, and she could only pray that this was a portent for the future. As carefully as if he was unwrapping a precious gift he slipped her bodice below her breasts and tenderly fondled her nipples. Kisses followed and Judith began to forget her doubts, the tension leaving her as she lay there languorously, enjoying his caresses. Her body, as if a thing apart that had recently shaken off restrictions, responded to him. She could hear herself almost purring, and ran her hands over his face and

94

throat, and tugged at his doublet, that naughty flesh of hers demanding to be pressed against his nakedness.

Mark was not to be hurried, however, relishing each step of the mating ritual, leading her little by little to the pinnacle. She marvelled at his control as he undressed her slowly, then removed his own clothes and, admiring every inch of her, concentrated on those sensitive areas that raised her higher and higher until she reached her first climax. Nipples, breasts, belly and sex, all received special attention and, while he roused her for the second time she boldly handled his phallus and testicles, marvelling at the feel of the masculine equipment.

Now love was blossoming in her heart, and this added to the ecstasy. She wanted this man in her life forever. When he entered her it was as if she found the part of herself that had always been missing, a complete unity of body and soul. She strained against him, impaling herself on his engorged member until his frantic thrusts and muttered expletives told her that he was reaching the point of no return. A hot flood of semen filled her, and she welcomed it as part of this man that she loved.

Later they dressed and he took her back to the bar, where he hired a boy to carry a flare before them and guide them to Antonia's house. The church clock chimed midnight as Mark kissed her and left her at the gate.

More days of learning to ride while wielding a sword, controlling the beast with the knees, and more hand to hand combat, more nights of sleeping in a tent, though by now Judith had found a palette and blankets. She and Tom compared notes whenever they met, and he glowed with pride at his achievements with the pike and musket, and boasted to the girls who managed the wagons. She had not seen Mark again.

Antonia, satisfied with the way she coped with the discomforts, gave her permission to use the guestroom again, saying, 'Tidy yourself this evening and come to my apartment. There's someone I want you to meet.'

Puzzled, Judith selected a clean shirt and breeches, topped by a plain doublet. She polished her boots until they shone, and then brushed her hair. She had lost weight and it suited her, and she postured before the mirror aping the affectations of the young men, standing with legs apart, hands in pockets or walking with a swagger. She buckled on her sword, used by now to the feel of it against her left thigh, and then left the room.

She heard a dog barking from within as she knocked on Antonia's door, followed by a strong, masculine voice shouting, 'Be quiet, Boye!'

On entering she saw them, the dog and the man. The former was a large white shaggy poodle, and its master the tallest, most striking person she had ever encountered. 'Come in, Judith,' Antonia said in greeting, then turned to the dog owner. 'Your Highness, may I present Lady Ashwell. I told you how she helped me escape.'

So this was Prince Rupert! Judith didn't know whether to bow or curtsey, so she did the first, hardly daring to meet his eyes, but when she did it was to find him observing her closely. She was very much in awe of him, his formidable reputation, his royal birth making him an almost godlike figure. But now he was smiling and chastening his dog, who was sniffing

Judith.

'Boye! Come here, sirrah! This is a friend.'

She was flattered, fascinated by his accent and awed by his presence. Greatly daring she patted the large, amiable animal, who was obviously devoted to his owner. 'Boye,' she ventured, patting his head while he tried to lick her fingers.

'He was given to me when I was a prisoner in Linz. My comrade then and ever since. He goes everywhere with me, even to King Charles's table, and he makes a great fuss of him.' Rupert's eyes sparkled with amusement as he played with his pet, who now rolled on his back so his stomach could be rubbed by the prince's booted foot.

This almost domesticated scene put Judith at ease. Generalissimo of the whole army he might be, but Rupert was also a young man who had only visited England once before when a boy, and was now responsible for the safety of his uncle and the outcome of the war.

'Good evening, Lady Ashwell,' said a familiar voice, and Mark appeared from the shadows.

This was almost too much. He was there, with his commander and, looking across at Antonia, she could tell by her smile that she had arranged this. There was something else, too. Judith had never seen her so vivacious and she was staring at Rupert constantly, her face alive with admiration. Was she in love with the prince? Surely not? Antonia never fell in love, did she?

'Be seated, Judith,' Antonia said. 'There are serious matters afoot. His Highness is marching North with as many men as he can muster. He intends to go to the aid of the Marquis of Newcastle and relieve York.'

Judith could not concentrate on the weighty matters under discussion, only conscious of Mark seated close to her by the table, where Rupert and Antonia were consulting a large map and planning routes. Mark's opinion was asked several times and he rose to lean across and give advice. When he moved away she felt momentarily bereft, happy again as she felt the pressure of his thigh against hers when he returned.

'We shall leave as soon as possible,' Rupert said decisively. 'I have left a force guarding Bristol and another to keep Oxford safe.'

'May I and my soldiers ride with you?' Antonia asked eagerly.

He nodded. 'Yes, and I shall gather more men as we march. I need as many as possible to swell the ranks.'

'We shall be proud to join in, Highness. Is it true that the queen is going to Exeter for the birth of her baby?'

'She has been advised to do so, and will stay with her friend, Lady Villiers, during the confinement. It will be safer there.'

All Judith could hear was the fact that he would be leaving and no doubt Mark as well. But she would be marching with Antonia, and might be able to see him. The thought of losing Mark made her feel hollow. She was desperate to spend one more hour with him. Antonia, too, seemed unusually agitated, whispering to her, 'Take Mark to your room. I need to be alone with His Highness.'

Judith managed to control herself until the door closed behind her and Mark. Then she let go and cried. He gathered her into his arms. 'What is it, sweetheart?'

'This war,' she sobbed. 'The upheaval of it all…'

'Consider the good side. We should never have met had it not happened.' He fished in his pocket for a handkerchief and wiped her tears.

'That's true.' Her sobs subsided, but she was still troubled. 'So, we shall be marching on the same campaign, but shall we be able to meet? You'll be in constant danger. I don't think I can endure it.'

'It is out of our hands,' he soothed, leading her to sit with him on the bed. He gave a sigh. 'I have been longing for this. When His Highness said where he was going tonight I had to come with him, just for the chance of seeing you.'

'But we shall be parted tomorrow.'

'Both of us travelling towards York. There may be a chance we can see each other on the way.' He smoothed the curls back from her brow. 'All is not lost. Let us make the most of what little time we have.' Then he smiled, and added, 'You make a most attractive lad, but I have never before been tempted by my own sex.'

'Nor will you now. This is but a masquerade. I'm all woman beneath. Let me show you.'

With fumbling fingers she stripped, baring herself for him. He watched her, then touched her shoulders and drifted down to her breasts, muttering, 'You are so beautiful. I want you for my own.'

She threw herself upon him. 'You can have me. I am yours.'

All doubts vanished. She no longer cared if this one night was all they would ever have. The present was all important and she wriggled against him, and then helped him out of his clothes. His muscular body thrilled her and she joyfully received his every caress,

99

no matter how intimate. His skilful handling of her most private parts brought her to heights she had never reached before, and this was because she loved him, her emotion expressed in a physical manner.

He was sensitive to her climax, letting her rest before carefully rousing her again, and this time she cried out, needing his cock in her vagina. He was there, plunging deeply, his phallus like a mighty spear impaling her. She yelled again and wanted to get closer and closer, wishing they could be absorbed into each other, body and soul united.

Antonia was content. To sit by the smouldering fire with Rupert, looking at maps, discussing strategy, fired by the one-pointed zeal of the man, was heaven for her. By now she knew about war, had taken part in battles gained by the Royalists, but Rupert was much more serious than before.

'Lord Digby and General Goring are thorns in my side,' he said angrily. 'They give the king bad advice.'

She was honoured to be in the position of his confidante. There weren't many people he trusted. His brother, Prince Maurice, was his devoted ally, so were his followers, and now herself. It seemed he inspired fervent admiration or violent dislike. There were no half measures with Rupert.

Boye growled, eyes closed, stretched out on the foot of the bed. Rupert went over and tumbled him off. 'You can't share my couch tonight.' The dog reluctantly occupied the hearthrug, and his master lay back, long limbs crossed, arms linked behind his head. 'My God, I'm tired. There's so much to do and the king surrounds himself with knaves and fools.'

Antonia stood beside him. 'Let's get those off,' and

as he presented one leg she took it between her own and hauled at the riding boot, managing to wrench it free, and then she tackled the second. He flopped back against the pillows with a sigh of relief.

She leaned over him. His eyes were closed, the lashes like fans against his cheek and he looked much younger. Kneeling there, still wearing her male clothing, she ran kisses over his face, neck and ears, pushing back the dark locks. He did not respond and she wondered if he was asleep. She unbuttoned his shirt and kissed his chest and beyond, following the line of crisp hair down past his navel, opening the flap of his breeches and exposing his groin. He stirred and gripped her, bringing her mouth ever closer to his erection. They did not speak as she explored him, tongue caressing the hard stem and lingering around the foreskin and helm. She was skilled in bringing those of either sex to their peak, and lavished all this knowledge on him.

She took him to the edge, over and over, then stopped while his hold on her tightened and he groaned with frustration. Antonia rejoiced as she heard the heavy beating of his heart and the slow gasps of his breathing, feeling him shudder and buck until that final moment when she relented and sucked hard, milking him of every drop of spunk. In that hour of passion his rank and royal birth could go hang. He was hers alone.

He was wide awake now and, as if in apology for not making love to her, said, 'Antonia, we're not on duty tonight, so let us undress and sleep together, as man and woman as well as comrades.'

She was touched, guessing how hard it was for him to put his feelings into words when he came to anything other than warfare. He was no gallant who wooed ladies, or swashbuckler who swept them off their feet. She was in a privileged position, and used this to show him how to make love to the satisfaction of both.

Judith was taking part in a battle that had started late in the day, in the midst of a thunderstorm. Her horse had been shot from under her and she had only just escaped being crushed beneath him as he fell in that turmoil of mud and rain, where men were dying.

She could hear their screams above the noise of thunder and cannon, and drums rolling in an attempt to rally the scattered soldiers to their standards. Lightening flashed on the chaotic scene, but she couldn't find Antonia or any members of her own troop. In that hell of smoke and death muskets rattled, horses bolted and the Royalists were facing defeat.

It had been so sudden and unexpected. They had settled down for the night, never thinking that anyone would attack so late in the day or in such weather. Judith had followed Antonia's commands, leaping on to her horse, having experienced skirmishes by now, and following her leader into the fray. She found herself alone, stumbling over corpses and her right arm was numb from parrying blows, remembering Sergeant Miller's instructions. As yet she had not killed anyone, but now to stay alive she had no choice.

A large figure wearing a pot helmet and orange sash reared up before her, his sword raised. Judith acted by instinct, ducking and lifting her weapon high, driving it into his throat. Blood gushed out, spraying her, mingling with the rain as a fork of lightning hit a tree. 'Oh, my God!' she yelled, Sergeant Miller's voice ringing in her ears. '*You won't think about killing. It will be him or you*!'

It was the first, but she had no time to dwell on it, survival all important. Two other men were coming towards her, stepping over their fallen comrade. They were grinning, swords at the ready. Judith tried to fight them but it was useless. They beat down her blade and grabbed her.

'God be praised!' shouted the burliest of them. 'This isn't a man. It's one of those she-soldiers! Witches who fuck the Devil Prince, Rupert!'

Even in the midst of battle their intentions were plain. They wanted to find a spot where they could rape her. One seized the neck of her shirt and ripped it down, exposing her breasts, and this seemed to drive them wild. They were both at her, handling her brutally, and she could feel herself falling, losing her footing in the mud. The men were on her. Stars danced before her eyes as something struck her on the brow. She could not get her balance but clung to her sword, slashing about wildly. Then it was gone, wrenched from her hand.

They were laughing. She could hear them even amidst the tumult. She was seized, lifted and carried to where a deserted wagon stood. The soldiers where clumsy in their eagerness to take her and then kill her. One held her while the other yanked down her breeches and tried to insert his cock into her. He did not succeed. Suddenly he started, reared backwards and then fell to the ground, a knife protruding from his back. His comrade spun round, but was too late. A sword plunged into his chest and was withdrawn with equal speed. He dropped like a sack of grain.

Judith was shaking violently, unable to believe it when Frankie appeared before her, saying, 'Let's get out of here. The Roundheads are winning.'

'Where is the prince?' Judith was dazed and confused, struggling to stand and pull up her breeches. Tom materialised beside her.

'I don't know. In the midst of it, I expect.'

'And Antonia?'

'Don't worry about her.' Frankie pulled the orange sashes from the dead Roundheads. 'Here, put one on.'

'I can't wear their colours!' Judith was appalled.

'Don't be a fool! We're in retreat and this may give us a chance of survival.' A new sound joined the deafening din of battle. Women were screaming, the cries of children mixed with them. 'Damn those bloody hypocrites! They've found the camp-followers.'

They could see the circle of wagons where those who had come to aid their men huddled. Flames leapt from the hooped canvas tops, black smoke rising.

'We can't help them, Frankie,' Tom said. 'There's nothing we can do.'

Frankie dragged at Judith's arm, heading for a ditch that was shielded by a hedge. They kept their heads down, making through the mud. It was getting darker, night clouds rushing in to augment those of the storm.

'God, what I'd give for dry clothes!' muttered Frankie, stumbling over a body, stopping to go through his pockets and take his sword. She handed it to Judith. 'You may need this.'

Judith grabbed it, but the feel of it in her hand appalled her; she had just killed a man with such a weapon. They floundered on, but just as they thought they could traverse the ditch and put it between themselves and the battlefield half a dozen mounted men caught up with them, shouting, 'Stop!'

Pistols were trained on them and Frankie muttered, 'Do as they say or we'll get our heads blown off.'

Their leader dismounted, a stout man whose eyes shone with a fanatical light. 'You're wearing our colours. To which regiment do you belong?'

'Oliver Cromwell's!' Frankie answered.

Their assailants laughed derisively and their commander came closer, eyeing her up and down, Judith too. 'I don't think so. He doesn't hold with women playing the soldier.' He grabbed her doublet and wrenched it open, displaying the outline of her breasts beneath her shirt.

She slapped his hand away and his face darkened. 'A spitfire, eh? And what about your little friend?'

'Leave them be, sir.' Tom took a stand in front of him. 'Take me prisoner, but let them go.'

'I don't think so. Such women are jezebels, an abomination in the sight of the Lord. They need to be punished. Is this not so, lads?'

'Aye, Captain Jennings, you never said a truer word!' shouted his men. Several of them dismounted and Tom was outnumbered, helpless in their hands.

Held captive Frankie put up a fight, but a blow across the face stopped her. Judith stood silent. This was like the worst kind of nightmare – the clamour of artillery, the scream and shouts and the never-ending claps of thunder. Jennings paced around his female prisoners, a slow, considering smile on his face.

He addressed his troopers. 'What shall we do with them, boys?'

'Strip them!' one suggested with a leer.

Jennings pulled a reproving face. 'Wouldn't this be a sin, exposing their nakedness?'

'No, sir. They're whores, and it is God's will that they be chastised.'

Jennings made no further protestations. In fact he was the first to tear off Judith's clothing, leaving her nude and shivering, trying to cover her breasts with one arm and her pubic mound with the other hand. The soldiers laughed and clamoured to touch her, while Frankie spat and fought to no avail. She, too, was stripped naked, standing barefoot in the rain. Tom was furious, but a pistol jammed into his ribs kept him quiet.

With the sound of battle fading into the distance Jennings handled Judith's breasts, while his men waited his instructions. 'I think it is my duty to make this one confess her sins,' he said slowly. 'I want a couple of you to hold her while I examine her to see if she's made like other women or has special qualities because she's a witch. I will search for teats in her private parts, where she suckles demons. After which I shall turn my attention to the other.'

Judith was gripped in tough hands, held firm by her arms and spread legs while Jennings released a large, fully erect penis. He inserted his fingers into her, feeling her lower lips and clitoris then delving into her vagina. He was grunting with pleasure while his men watched, each of them expressing excitement.

'Let her go, you canting pig of a Puritan!' Frankie demanded, but was silenced by a hand clapped over her mouth.

Jennings ignored her. 'I shall have to go further,' he said, his voice shaking. 'Though threatening my place in heaven it is my duty to explore her depths, even if it harms my manhood.'

Judith shut her eyes tightly, wanting to blot out the sight of this awful man taking hold of his phallus and guiding it into her. She felt it forcing its way into her dry passage and a scream formed on her lips.

Then suddenly she heard a voice shouting, 'Jennings! What are you doing? Let that woman go!'

He was forcibly removed. She opened her eyes to see another group of horsemen, and for a second thought they had been rescued by Royalists, then their leader swung down and her worst fears became reality.

Jennings and his men stood back, and she heard the newcomer approaching. He stood there staring at her, and said in a familiar voice, 'How dare you touch this woman?'

'She's worth nothing, an immodest she-soldier fighting for the king. I'm sure she's a witch and was looking for marks on her body,' Jennings blurted.

To her horror Judith focused on Steven, who was glaring at her as he said, 'I will take charge of these prisoners. This lady, if she so calls herself, is my runaway wife.'

Chapter 6

Antonia guessed it was all over. She had never before witnessed such a catastrophic defeat. The Parliamentarians had taken unfair advantage of the storm and approaching night but, she recollected ruefully, all's fair in love and war, and the enemy were much better organised now.

She was weaving through the combatants, trying to gather her scattered troops. She found some but there was no sign of Judith, Frankie or Tom. 'Where is Prince Rupert?' she shouted as one of his men passed her.

'Last seen attempting to round up his cavalry. I'm getting out of here while I can,' and he disappeared in the opposite direction to the mêlée.

Still beating off attackers she could hardly see anything, apart from the lightning and burst of fire from artillery and guns. Self-preservation forced her to make for the darker hump of forest in the distance. She passed many Royalists taking the same direction, their one thought that of escape, and this was paramount, even above the horror of realising that they had lost the battle.

Judith was roped to the side of Steven's mount, compelled to keep up, splashing through the mud, shivering with cold with only the cloak covering her. Everywhere triumphant Roundheads were cheering, taking prisoners, looting and abusing the women in the Royalist camp. It was as Judith had suspected; though spouting religion their behaviour was no better than any other army. Frankie and Tom were near her, forced to tramp along by their guards' horses. Judith was so weary she could not think of the nasty possibilities of what Steven intended to do with her. All she wanted was rest, and eventually they reached the camp set up before they made their unexpected attack.

Steven halted, dismounted and propelled her into a large tent. There he chained her to a pole, muttering, 'I shall return shortly.'

'My friends,' she stammered. 'What will become of them?'

'I haven't made up my mind about the girl. I may keep her hostage, but Tom Maslin will hang tomorrow, along with other prisoners.'

'Not Tom! Please, Steven, be merciful! He was one

108

of your own grooms, brought up at Ferris Mead. You can't see him hanged.'

'He is a traitor!' His eyes blazed with fanatical fire. 'All traitors to the Parliament deserve death. Soon Prince Rupert's head will adorn a pike on London's Tower Bridge, and even the king will be dealt with severely.'

Despair swamped her as he stormed out and she was left in darkness. He had removed the cloak before chaining her, and the cold was eating into her bones. She could hear noises from outside; men talking, shouting, laughing, celebrating their victory. Throughout the journey from Oxford, and the relief of York, none of the Royalists had dreamed that they would suffer such a defeat. Judith had become toughened throughout the trek, putting her new skills into practice, but up until then it had almost seemed to be a game. Now she was facing grim reality. She had killed a man. Would his ghost haunt her? And where was Antonia? And was Mark lying dead on the battlefield?

She was beyond tears, slumped against the tent pole, the manacles digging into her wrists, praying that Steven would not return, but it seemed that God had deserted her. He lifted the canvas flap and came in, carrying a lamp.

He stood in front of her, shining the light in her face. 'Well, what have you to say for yourself?' he demanded.

She out-stared him. 'Nothing.'

His lip curled in a sneer. 'Nothing? After what you have done? Helping a prisoner, running off with her, tempting a lad to aid you? Fighting for the Royalists? May God forgive you, for I never shall.' He hung the lamp on a hook.

'You don't understand...'she began.

'Understand? Oh, I understand well enough. You are a wanton hussy who doesn't merit the name of Ashley. Were I not a magnanimous man I should have our marriage annulled on the grounds of adultery.'

'Do so,' she pleaded. 'I no longer want to be tied to you.'

His slap across the face knocked her head against the post. 'Be silent, whore! Your wants are of no consequence,' he barked. 'I am your master and shall deal with you as I think fit.'

Judith could taste the blood on her split lip and accepted that he was beyond reason. She was helpless. His hands were roaming over her body, seeking out her most private places as if she really did belong to him.

'Don't touch me!' she shouted, and spat in his face.

He wiped away the spittle and then squeezed her breasts painfully, muttering, 'You will regret that.'

He unlocked the chains and flung her to the earth floor. Her wrists were still manacled and she crouched there, helpless. He rested his booted foot in the small of her back and pressed down, grinding in his heel. Then, bending, he grabbed a handful of her hair and hauled her up against him.

She glared into his eyes. 'You call yourself a godly man. Let me go free and I'll make sure we are divorced and never see each other again.'

He laughed and released her. She heard a swish and pain burned through her as his whip landed on her bare skin. 'You won't get away from me, and I'll spend the rest of my days punishing you. It's my duty to transform you into an obedient wife. Think of this while you await my return. I must leave you now.

There is much to do before we can rest, rounding up prisoners, burying our dead, caring for the wounded, making certain that the Royalists have left the moor. This done, I shall be back.'

He chained her to the post again, with her face against the hard wood, and went out, taking the lantern with him. Judith was plunged into darkness again. Her skin burned where he had struck her. She was shivering with cold and shock, terrified, too. Steven was capable of any cruelty. She felt there were no more tears left in her, and slumped there. Despite pain and despair she was exhausted and sleep overcame her.

A sound brought her sharply awake. It was still dark. Male hands gripped her and she felt the press of a strong body and caught a whiff of Steven's sweat. She yelped as he pressed himself against her whipped flesh, and cried out again when he forced her thighs apart and began trying to insert his penis into her rectum.

'Don't! Stop!' she screamed.

He did so, and for a moment she imagined that he was being merciful. Then she gasped as his whip cut across her buttocks, followed by another blow, and another. In that hell of agony she tried to turn her head and see him, but it was impossible.

'Have you had enough?' he grated. 'Are you prepared to carry out your wifely duty?'

'No!' She was still defiant. 'If you force me it will be rape.'

His harsh laughter rang through the tent. 'A man can't rape his own wife.'

He was there again, guiding his erection to her anus. She sensed he would not be content with her vagina. It was his desire to inflict as much suffering on her as he could. What he had said was true; there was no law protecting wives. They were the property of their husbands. Nevertheless, Judith put up a fight, struggling, kicking out, but to no avail. Although Steven tried to moisten his cock at her crack she was bone dry. He cursed and spat on his hand, applying it to her anal opening, then thrusting hard.

It was an agonising experience. Judith had never known such treatment. It was as if she was being disembowelled. Then, with a final mighty push, he succeeded in entering her. Once her inner muscles had stretched to receive him the pain lessened and she felt powerful, clenching hard.

'Supposing I don't let go?' she hissed. 'You could be trapped within me.' She gave his organ an extra squeeze. 'How would that appear to your followers, if they found you in such a position?'

'I'd kill you first,' he threatened, panting heavily. 'A corpse would have no hold on me.' But her words had cost him dear and his cock softened, allowing him to withdraw without taking his pleasure to the full.

Instead he picked up his crop and beat her savagely, then wrapped his cloak around himself, lay on the floor and was silent. Almost hysterical, Judith started to laugh in spite of the pain and discomfort in which she passed what remained of the night.

The morning brought news. A solider shouted from outside the tent, 'Captain Ashley! Two of the prisoners escaped in the dark.'

'What?' Steven was awake and on his feet in an instant. He flung back the tent flap. 'Which ones?'

'Those we took with your wife, sir. A she-soldier and a young man.'

Tom and Frankie! Judith's heart leapt with joy, but she kept it from Steven.

He swung round on her, shouting, 'What do you know about this?'

'Nothing,' she answered truthfully.

'If I find out it was your doing…' he threatened.

'What will you do? Hang your own wife? That would be well received by our villagers, I'll wager,' she mocked, though well aware of the messenger eyeing her nakedness.

'I'll head a search party, and then we're marching back to Ferris Mead at once.'

'Release me first, I need my cloak,' she said in a clear, controlled voice.

'Very well, but I shall leave you under guard, and they will have orders to kill you should you try to run away.'

Rumours were rife in Oxford. Antonia reached there after a gruelling journey. Gradually scattered forces from the battle had joined up together, and she and her remaining troopers were among them, but there was no sign of Judith.

She arrived at Isobel's house, dishevelled and dirty and tired out. She had met up with Jamie on the way. He was pale and weak and had lost blood from a wound in his thigh. She had done what she could for him and handed him over to the baroness.

'Come in, come in! I was afraid I would never see either of you again.' Isobel called for her maid and ordered warm water, and salves and linen, and had a footman bring up food and wine. She went on talking as she dressed Jamie's wound. 'Oxford is in a wax. Rumours are flying that Cromwell intends to attack it following his success in the North. The queen gave birth to a baby daughter in Exeter and later fled to France, leaving the infant with Lady Villiers.'

'Where is Prince Rupert? Is it true that a Roundhead put a bullet in Boye?' Antonia asked, having heard about this and praying that it was false information.

'Yes, they killed him and are boasting about it in their broadsheets. Rupert has gone to his headquarters in Shrewsbury. Apparently he blames himself, for in the sudden confusion when the enemy attacked without warning he forgot to tie Boye to a wagon and the faithful creature followed him into battle.'

Boye was dead. Antonia could only imagine Rupert's distress. This, coupled with his defeat, was enough to shake even his confidence. She longed to be beside him, offering her support.

She sank her teeth into a slice of chicken breast. Food had been hard to come by on the way there, although she had money, but had been wary of putting up in a tavern for the night in case the landlord was a Parliament supporter. She had slept in empty barns or copses, resting Sultan, thankful to still have him. She ached in every bone, relishing the feel of a cushioned chair under her, and the warmth of a fire. Safe, too, without being constantly on the alert, but she was concerned for Judith.

'Ah, God, but that's so good,' sighed Jamie, relaxing under Isobel's ministrations. 'I think I'll leave the army. I've had enough.'

'You're jesting, of course,' she reprimanded. 'None of us can abandon His Majesty's cause. D'you think I want to live under Puritan rule, with no parties, no maypoles, no Christmas or fine clothes or fun of any kind? I'd rather take up arms myself.' She paused at a hammering at the door, and then called out, 'Who is it?'

'Two soldiers, my lady,' a footman answered. 'They are begging audience.'

'Bid them enter.'

Antonia swung round, astonished and delighted when a travel-stained Frankie and Tom came in. 'Thank God! Where is Judith? Is she with you?'

'No, no. She was captured by her husband. We all were, and I was to be hanged,' Tom babbled, words tumbling over one anther. 'But we managed to kill our guards, steal their money, clothes and horses, and escape.'

'Judith is still with him. He is heading for their home, Ferris Mead, where he promises to humiliate and punish her,' Frankie butted in. 'We came straight here, thinking we might find you and maybe organise an attack on his manor house. We must get her away from him.'

Isobel pushed them into chairs and gave them food and drink, while Antonia rose, pacing the floor like a caged beast. 'Indeed, we must. She can't be left to the mercies of that man. From what I've seen of him, added to her tales of his cruelty, it is essential that we act soon.' She drove her fist into her palm. 'But I must see the prince first, and get his permission. I'll ride for Shrewsbury tomorrow. Meanwhile, we should all rest.'

'Come to bed with me, Antonia, and I'll arrange a room for you, Frankie and Tom. Seek what comfort you can together, whether it is friendship with a dash of coupling, or just comradely rapport.'

Jamie had already fallen asleep on the couch, and Isobel covered him, tender as a mother, and then led Antonia into the dressing-room where a tub stood, filled with warm water. They bathed together, soaping each other and then caressing. Antonia's weariness vanished and she wanted more and more of the beautiful baroness. Men were all very well, but the softness and scent of women, their grace and understanding of female sexuality, thrilled her more.

The water sloshed gently around them and she dipped a hand beneath it, finding Isobel's sex and relishing the feel of the wet pubic hair, the soft vaginal wings and the swollen clitoris standing proud. Isobel sighed with pleasure and fondled Antonia's breasts, then leaned forward and kissed the nipples. Their mouths met, lips parted and tongues exploring, and then they rose, reaching for towels and returning to the bedroom.

It was wonderfully intimate, with its draped four-poster and luxurious surroundings. For a while they could forget everything, even ignoring the presence of Jamie, deeply asleep before the fire. They dried each other's hair and anointed their skin with perfumed lotion, and all the while their passion mounted.

'Ah, my warrior, how handsome you are, and so brave,' Isobel crooned, tweaking Antonia's nipples.

Antonia shook out her hair. It covered her shoulders and fell across her breasts. 'War isn't a game any more, Isobel. It is becoming deadly serious, and Judith is out there somewhere, a prisoner to her husband.'

'I know. I'm not a fool. The courtiers are panicking and the city uneasy, but let us not worry about that now. All we can do is pray that Judith is safe. You will see Rupert and hope that he agrees to an attack on Ferris Mead.' As she spoke, Isobel pressed Antonia against the pillows and leaned over her, kissing her face and neck, and tonguing her breasts and waist, belly and mound, wooing her into silence, and acceptance of the here and now.

Antonia welcomed this homage, nerves and senses responding, and returning the pleasure, her hands worshipping the sinuous curves and secret places of Isobel's body. There was no rush, no hurry as there might have been with a rampant male. They had time in which to enjoy the stirring up of desire, until both were ready to achieve the pinnacle of bliss. Lying side by side they explored their partner's nakedness, kissing and caressing and exposing swollen nubbins.

They murmured love words, complimented each other, and finally, completely roused, settled down to bring about mutual orgasms. Antonia opened her legs wide, exposing herself completely, and Isobel did the same. Then, half sitting, half lying, each fondled the other's crack, dipping into the copious dew and spreading it over the labia and finally settling on the clitoris. Now there was no stopping them, each gasping as the sensation mounted. They rubbed it in the same way that they did when masturbating, but this time it was almost better, their cries adding to the excitement.

Their climaxes came simultaneously, shuddering and gasping and arching their bodies against those wonderful fingers, then collapsing in each other's arms, completely satisfied.

'Would that life was always like this,' Isobel whispered, one hand still cupping Antonia's mound. 'Such peace and tranquillity.'

'Perhaps we should get bored after a while.' Antonia's mind was already streaking ahead to the task of riding to Shrewsbury.

She dreaded what sort of a mood she would find

117

Rupert in. Robbed of his dog and thrashed by his enemies, defeat would not sit easily on him. But it must be done. She owed it to Judith to save her from the clutches of her husband.

Lampton Village had not altered. Judith went through it towards Ferris Mead, seated side-saddle on the back of Steven's mount. The journey had taken several days, and he made it as uncomfortable for her as possible. She was constantly under guard, even when needing privacy to relieve herself. He made her beg for food and water, constantly humiliating her. She dreaded arriving at what had once been her home.

It was early evening when they rode up the drive towards the turreted building. Servants were lined on the front steps to greet their master. Judith saw Mrs Moffat staring at her, alongside Mr Barnes. What lies had they spread about her? She guessed she couldn't expect any help from either of them.

Steven reined in his horse and dismounted. He did not offer her a hand, and she dropped to the ground, wearing the overlarge black dress he had provided, covered with a cloak. His fingers held her arm in an iron grip as he led her forward. He paused when he reached the top of the steps, turning to dismiss his soldiers and then addressing the silent members of staff.

'God be praised! We beat the Royalists in the last battle!'

A cheer arose and Mrs Moffat curtsied, saying, 'We heard rumours of this, my lord. It was well done.' She continued to stare at Judith.

'We beat the Devil Prince and, amongst the foes, I found Lady Ashley, who has disgraced my name.

You will follow my orders regarding her.'

On every side Judith met blank faces, except for Mrs Moffat who did not try to conceal her disapproval. She had no idea what Steven intended to do, but her worst fears were realised when he walked her down to the dungeons in the bowels of the mansion. He unlocked a barred door and pushed her inside.

'You can't mean to leave me here,' she protested, glancing around the cheerless damp cell.

He smiled tauntingly. 'What did you expect? That I should have you back in the master bedchamber? A whore like you, who has been coupling with the enemy soldiers, women as well as men? I may do, if it suits me, but meanwhile you will stay here until I have decided what to do with you. And I expect you to be dutiful when I demand my conjugal rights.' He went out, locking the door behind him.

Judith stood in the centre of the cell, looking around her. The only light was from a window high up in the stone wall, and this was protected by iron bars. There was no bed, no chair, nothing, and if Steven intended to force himself on her, then it would have to be against the wall or on the bare brick floor. Did he want to starve her into submission, seeing her grovel? His behaviour suggested he would. She had hurt his pride, and this was all important to him.

Desperately weary she wanted to cry, but would not give him the satisfaction. She longed for Mark, and prayed for a miracle so that he might get her out of this dreadful prison. Frankie and Tom had escaped, and she took heart from this. If they had been able to link up with Antonia then surely she would devise some way of attacking Ferris Mead and freeing her?

She heard a key in the lock and saw Mrs Moffat through the bars. There was an unpleasant smile on her face as she entered and said, 'I've been ordered to bring you blankets, and a bucket for the relief of nature. Here's some bread and cheese. The master may decide to give you dinner later. I await his instructions. Meanwhile, you are under guard. There will be a man constantly on duty.'

Judith glanced across and saw him outside, leering at her. 'Am I to have no privacy?' she demanded, recalling that this unpleasant woman was no more than a servant.

'I do what the master tells me,' Mrs Moffat sneered. 'You gave up the right to call yourself mistress when you ran off with that trollop.'

'Supposing I tell him that you and Mr Barnes help yourselves to his wine when he's absent?' Judith refused to be browbeaten.

'He wouldn't believe you.' Mrs Moffat dropped the blankets and set the bucket in a corner. 'You betrayed him, and don't expect any support from me.'

She slammed out and the guard peered between the bars, mocking her and saying, 'Anything I can do for you, deary? What dirty games did you play with those Cavaliers, eh? You can tell me. I won't peach on you.'

'Go away!' she shouted, and hung one of the blankets over the door. Better to be cold than spied upon.

She ate the bread rapidly and drank some water. The time dragged and she was alert for every sound, hearing the guard greeting the one who came to take his place. Evening was drawing in. She could tell by the movement of light across the window, and then Mrs Moffat appeared again, bringing a lamp.

'The master has sent for you. Come at once.'

With the guard on one side and Mrs Moffat on the other, Judith was escorted aloft. Though suspicious of what Steven intended almost anything was preferable to that dismal cell.

They passed through the Great Hall and mounted the stairs, not stopping until they stood outside the master chamber. Mrs Moffat knocked and Steven's voice answered from within. 'Enter.'

Judith was pushed through the door, coming face to face with him. He jerked his head at Mrs Moffat and the guard. 'Leave us.'

The room was as she remembered it, living again those unhappy hours during which she had shared the bed with him. He let her wait; fearful of his intentions, then he went to the wardrobe, opened it and displayed her clothing, just as she had left it.

'You kept them!' she exclaimed.

He smiled mockingly. 'Of course I kept them. I had the gut feeling that you would return one day, and I've been prepared for you.'

'Not a pleasant welcome,' she snapped.

His smile vanished. 'Do you want a taste of the dungeon again? Be careful what you say. I am master.'

Judith curbed her tongue, asking, 'Why have you brought me here?'

He came closer, holding her at arm's length and studying her face. 'Matters have changed somewhat. I have been ordered away again, and shall be joined by Colonel Bennet. Together we shall be subduing the West Country. I've just had a message from him. He doesn't want to leave his wife, Lady Felicity, alone, and has asked me if she can stay with you, along with her own servants. Therefore, not wishing

121

to involve them in this sorry story concerning yourself, I am forced to permit you to resume your place as mistress here. But you will be watched closely. Mrs Moffat has her instructions.'

Judith inclined her head. 'Very well, sir. When are they arriving?'

'In a few days.' His arms came round her and, though she tried to hold away from him, he was insistent. 'Tonight you will have a thorough wash, for you stink, and then occupy your rightful place beside me in the marriage bed. I shall indulge my whim and observe you at your ablutions.'

The tub was ready before the fire and at any other time she would have relished the experience, but not with Steven sitting close by and watching her every movement. But there was nothing else for it, so she undressed and stepped into the water, sitting down as quickly as she could, her knees under her chin. There was plain soap and a cloth and she even managed to wash the sweat and dirt from her hair, almost forgetting Steven's presence.

Then he spoke. 'I have never seen a woman bathing before. There is a grace and beauty there that pleases me, especially as it is to be mine shortly.'

Judith tossed back her hair and glanced at him. His breeches were undone and he was handling his hard cock, pulling back the foreskin and smoothing the jism over the helm. It was a sight that disgusted her. He had upbraided her for touching her sexual parts, but he did so to his own.

He saw her watching him and slid down in the chair, giving her a clearer view of his equipment. She wanted to look away, but was compelled to watch. Had it been Jamie or Mark she might have found it stimulating, but this was an unkind, prejudiced, middle-aged man, with none of their dash and élan.

'What do you think of that?' he asked eagerly, handling his testicles. 'Were any of your Cavaliers so well endowed?'

She refused to answer, rinsing off the soap and rising, reaching for a towel. 'Don't cover yourself,' he ordered, and stood, still exposed. 'I want you naked and wet. Fight me if you like; this only makes the conquest sweeter.'

She glanced towards the door. But where could she run? There was nowhere to hide. She could do nothing but submit to him, and this wasn't easy when she disliked him so much. His very touch sickened her. He sensed it, and his smile deepened. He didn't want her to feel anything but revulsion. He forced her across the bed, raised his hand and brought it down mercilessly on her bare hinds. He struck her several times and then, using all his strength, entered her unwilling body.

Chapter 7

It was a long distance, mostly cross-country, to reach the town to which Rupert had retreated. Antonia planned the route carefully and dressed accordingly. It was dangerous to wear anything that hinted at association with the military. The rural folk were furious at being constantly pillaged by troops of either side, their cattle driven away, their poultry stolen. They had armed themselves with clubs and beat off anyone who was not a civilian.

Antonia enlisted the services of Frankie and Tom.

She dressed as a farmer's wife and they pretended to be her servants. She made up a story that she was on her way to visit a sick relative. She left Sultan in Oxford, intending to change horses daily at inns on the way. Accustomed though she was to hours in the saddle even her stamina was put to the test after so much fighting and riding. By the time they reached Shrewsbury and found the house of Mr Jones, with the Palatine colours floating over the chimney pots, she wanted to get the matter over and be on her way to rescue Judith.

The first person she met in the hallway was Mark, whose face lit up. 'Antonia! Where's Judith?'

'She was captured by her husband, of all people, and he's taken her back to Ferris Mead. I've come to see the prince and get his permission to besiege the house and get her away from him.'

'I'll be with you.'

'Where is Prince Rupert?'

'In his room drinking, I suspect.'

'Rupert? Drinking? I don't believe it.'

'He has taken the blame of the defeat on himself. You know how proud he is. And then there was the death of his dog… this was a blow to the heart.'

'Take me to him, and see that Frankie and Tom are fed and rested.'

She followed him up the staircase and met Rupert's valet at the door of his room. 'He has said not to be disturbed,' he faltered, trying to bar her way.

'Oh, for Heaven's sake, man, stand aside!' she shouted. 'Don't you remember me? I'm Captain Durward. Don't be deceived by my garb.'

Mark detained her momentarily, asking anxiously, 'We shall rescue Judith, shan't we?'

'I'll do my best,' and Antonia turned the handle

and went inside.

The curtains were drawn, a single candle burned on the table and the air was stale. A quick glance at the bed showed Rupert sprawled across it with a girl bending over him. He was muttering to her, and Antonia knew enough German to understand that he was ordering her to suck his cock.

Disgust and jealous rage made her seize the whore by the scruff of the neck and drag her off. Another, lying on his other side, shouted, 'What you playing at, missus? He's not paid us yet.'

'You expect to be paid by His Highness?' Antonia wanted to hit her, this camp harlot who'd had access to Rupert's body. 'Get out, both of you! Here,' she drew coins from her purse and threw them at her, 'there's your pay!'

Pocketing the money and tossing their heads they left the room. Antonia went to the window and opened it. The room was in a mess, and so was Rupert. She ordered his valet to bring water, and then help her wash the prince. He was unshaven and unkempt.

The valet was apologetic. 'I tried to make him see sense, madam, but he refused to listen, doing nothing but drink and have those hussies or others like them in here. Not at all like His Highness. I expect you've heard about Boye?' There were tears in his eyes.

'Yes, I heard. Help me get him into a clean shirt.'

He was heavy and dead drunk, unable to help himself, but once started Antonia refused to give up, and even managed to change the sheets and pillow cases. He fell back sound asleep, and she covered him with a blanket.

'Is there anything else, my lady?' The valet gathered up the soiled linen.

'No, I'll watch by him. Just see that my companions are looked after.'

'Yes, my lady. Will you call me when he recovers? He needs a shave.' The valet looked worried. He was used to keeping the prince smartly turned out.

She nodded, and could hardly wait to get rid of him, needing to be alone with Rupert, to rest by him and be the first person he saw on waking.

Drifting off to sleep despite her concerns about Judith she knew an odd kind of peace, resting close to him. There was always the intense relief because he had not been captured by the enemy. His escapes were almost miraculous and she could understand why they thought he had magical powers. But she knew him to be human, subject to the disappointments and frustrations that plague all mortals.

Eventually she heard him rise and use the chamber-pot, and then he stood by the bed, blinking and staring down at her. 'How did you get here?' he asked.

She sat up and held out her arms to him. 'I rode all the way to find you,' she said. 'Come, lie with me and I'll tell you about it.'

He rubbed his eyes, bewildered. 'Christ, my head aches.'

She made no comment, guessing that when he came to himself fully he would feel bad enough without her adding her piece.

He listened while she talked, then said, 'I'm recruiting again and building up a new train of artillery. I can't spare any soldiers to help your friend.'

She swallowed her disappointment. 'What if I take my own troop?'

He shook his head. 'I need them with me, and you.'
He came to rest beside her, his head on her shoulder.
'Can't we talk of something else? I feel most
damnably low.'

Antonia wanted to shake him and love him all at
the same time. She understood that he was hard
pressed to get his forces together again and she must
bite on the bullet and obey him, hoping against all
hope that Judith would be resourceful and find her
own way back. Perhaps Mark might be able to
persuade the prince to let him go. Meanwhile there
was their leader needing to be brought back to the
fostering of the cause.

She started to tell him about her own adventures in
the field and after, and he exploded in rage
concerning the dastardly way in which the enemy had
attacked, though conceding, 'That new man,
Cromwell, has the makings of a first-class
commander. Damned if he isn't copying my own
tactics and cavalry charges.' Then he broke off,
staring into space before adding, 'They killed Boye.'

She gripped his hand. 'I know.'

'There was no need for them to do that. How could
he harm them, a faithful beast who followed me into
battle? I should have tied him up, but it all happened
so quickly.'

'I know,' she said again, lost for words, feeling his
pain as acutely as if it was her own.

'And the king is blaming me for the defeat.'

This brought home to her more than anything just
how young he was, easily hurt despite his apparent
confidence, loving his uncle and wanting desperately
to regain his kingdom for him. All she could do was
offer him her loyal support. To confess her feelings
for him was out of the question, but she could

comfort him with her body, and began to do so, caressing his face and smoothing his hair. She paused, waiting for his reaction, and was pleased when he held her tightly and returned her kisses. Glad that the valet had washed his master's private parts she was eager to banish any trace of the whores, and unfastened his shirt and breeches.

He made no protest, and Antonia stripped off her own clothes, and taking his hands, laid them on her breasts. His response was immediate. He lowered his head and sucked her nipples into even harder peaks. She fondled his phallus, which had risen above his navel. He moaned and kicked off his breeches, freeing that formidable weapon.

With a knee between hers he opened her legs and was about to enter her when she stopped him, saying gently, 'Not yet, Highness. Play with me first,' and once again she showed him how to stimulate her clitoris.

Impetuous though he might be in battle, he remembered what she had taught him before, schooling his desire until she had reached orgasm. Then he took her as forcefully as when he was leading a cavalry charge and she relished the strength and passion of her Devil Prince.

Judith was permitted to wear her own clothes, taken from the armoire and the tallboy drawers. She had expected to be returned to the dungeons, but it seemed that Steven had other plans, wanting to impress Colonel Bennet. Loathsome though it was to share a bed with him she did not protest, knowing it would have been useless, and aware that she might have become seriously ill down there in the cold.

Mrs Moffat was in complete charge of the

household now, never referring to Judith. She was in her element, worse than even before, bullying the maidservants, using her cane on them mercilessly and ignoring Judith when she remonstrated. The men came under the jurisdiction of Mr Barnes and he was strict enough, but nothing like the tyrannical Mrs Moffat.

In the old days Judith had hardly ever argued with her, but had been given a certain status now removed. She was a puppet mistress with no power, always conscious of the woman spying and reporting her every movement or utterance to Steven.

The first few days were exceedingly difficult. Steven lost no opportunity to humiliate her in front of everyone. She was not permitted to set foot outside, confined to the bedroom unless escorted to the solar, where she was allowed to work at her embroidery frame. Newly accustomed to a life of activity and travel, boredom reduced her to almost screaming pitch. Her thoughts ran to Antonia and Frankie and, above all, Mark. Where were they? Did they know of her plight? She spent hours fretting over plans of escape, but guessed that she'd been first time lucky and that it was unlikely to happen again.

The days were better than the nights, for Steven seemed to be insatiable, his lust for punishment as great as that for copulation, and this was all she could call it, for there was no love or tenderness involved. She simply closed her eyes and thought of Mark, although by now he seemed a distant, beautiful dream.

One morning, after being awake for some time listening to the sounds of the servants going about their duties, and Steven's snores, she could stand it no more, risking a beating by shaking him and snapping, 'How much longer am I to endure this treatment?'

He started up, an unpleasant sight with his stubbly jaw and sparse hair. 'What ails you, woman? How dare you give me such a rude awakening?'

She leapt from the bed, a naked termagant, hands on her hips. Let him do his worst! 'I'm sick and tired of being treated with scorn by everyone. You have no right to do this. If you can't give me back my rights as mistress here then let me go. I'll trouble you no more.'

He was up in a flash, ridiculous in his crumpled nightshirt. He seized her, shook her, and marched her to the bed. There he ripped off the curtain cords and lashed her wrists to the post. She kicked out but he soon had her ankles tethered. Then he stood back, smiling grimly.

'You have no right to demand anything. I shall do with you as I wish. Colonel Bennet and his entourage will be arriving today, so you need something to remind you that I demand impeccable behaviour.' He strode to the door and shouted, 'Mrs Moffat!'

This was the last straw. Judith swore like a fishwife, shouting and cursing. Mrs Moffat appeared, cast one glance at her and said, 'What can I do for you, my lord?'

'Her ladyship is demanding more freedom,' he answered coldly, flicking his whip over Judith's thighs.

'But this is against your wishes, isn't it, my lord?' Mrs Moffat was watching the path of that vicious strip of leather with interest. 'I thought you had given orders that she was not to be obeyed or allowed out of the house.'

'That is correct.' Almost caressingly he trailed the

whip over Judith's bare breasts and across her belly, ending where the thatch of fair hair covered her pubis. 'You have played your part, I presume, issuing orders to members of the household?'

'I have, sir. They dare not disobey me.'

'I'm glad to hear it. As you know we are expecting company. I must prepare to meet them but Lady Judith needs reprimanding, so can I leave the task to you? Six stokes, I think.' He went to hand the whip to Mrs Moffat.

'It will be a pleasure, your lordship.' She hesitated, then said, 'Might I use my cane, sir? It proves mighty effective with the maids.'

'Certainly, and when I am ready I shall return and perform my husbandly duty. It is necessary that we have an heir. Do you understand?'

'Perfectly, sir.' There was a panting eagerness about Mrs Moffat that Judith found most offensive.

'You can't really be ordering this menial to cane me?' she gasped indignantly.

'You deserve no better.' He thrust his face close to hers. 'I'll have no more of your defiance, madam. Is that understood? If it happens again I'll have you flogged in front of all the staff, no matter how lowly their station.'

He stalked into the dressing-room, after summoning his manservant, who passed Judith with a smirk. Mrs Moffat approached her, grinning as she raised the cane. It landed across Judith's stomach and she could not restrain a cry. Another followed, but she would not let Mrs Moffat see how much she was suffering. Looking at her, trying to shame her into stopping, it was obvious that she was excited by her task. There was sweat beading her upper lip and the smell of arousal wafting from her. Memories of

Isobel's orgy flashed through Judith's brain. There she had learned that some like using the whip while others found satisfaction in being the victim. Mrs Moffat was one of the former, despite her Puritan ways.

The pain was becoming unendurable and Judith writhed in her bonds, but there was no relief until her tormenter counted six. Then the cords were untied and Judith, still retaining her pride, sat on the edge of the bed. She would not give Mrs Moffat the enjoyment of seeing her examine the red stripes that marred her skin.

The woman laid down the cane, still sweating and panting, her voice almost reverent as she said, 'His lordship will be back shortly.'

Judith glared at her, hissing, 'Why don't you bed him? It's plain that is what you want. Have him. Take him. He is no use to me.'

'That is a wicked thing to say!' Mrs Moffat was so indignant that Judith thought she was about to seize the cane and strike her again.

'Well, surely you should know by now that I am very, very wicked,' Judith scoffed. 'I've met the Devil Prince himself, and his dog Boye, until some bastard Roundhead shot the harmless animal.'

Mrs Moffat shuddered and Judith smiled wryly. 'If you had been a Catholic you would have crossed yourself at the mention of his name.'

'The master is right when he says you are dangerous.' Mrs Moffat raised her voice in indignation. 'Those evil Royalists have corrupted you. It is only through his mercy that you are still alive.'

Judith was recovering, though her body still throbbed. She chose to ignore the housekeeper's last taunt. 'Fetch my clothes,' she ordered, as if the incident had never happened. 'And have hot water brought up. Prepare the wash basin and I need soap.'

'Don't obey her, Mrs Moffat.' Steven came in at that moment, fully attired. 'Leave us now. I will take care of madam.' She scuttled out with a backward sneering glance at Judith. He walked over to where she sat. 'Still defiant, wife? I see that you haven't yet learnt your lesson. My guests will be here this afternoon, so there is still time for further taming.'

She wished so much that she possessed the muscles of a man as he held her and forced his mouth down on hers, his tongue parting her lips. She twisted away but he dragged her to the side-table and pushed her over it brutally, face down, arms spread out and her nakedness on display. A blow across the head stunned her and he pushed a hand between her buttocks, opening her to his gaze. Regaining her senses she continued to struggle, but could feel his naked cock against her vagina.

Expecting him to thrust she braced herself, but he raised his hand and she yelped as he spanked her vulnerable buttocks. The imprint of his palm was like a brand burning into her. Her cry roused him to a frenzy and he spanked her again and again. She sagged across the table's surface and he could hold back no longer, pushing his organ into her dry channel and taking his fill of her.

Colonel Bennet was a big bluff man who reminded Judith of a Cavalier rather than a Parliamentarian. He was several years his wife's senior, and she watched him with devoted eyes as they entered the great hall to be welcomed by Steven and Judith.

'Ah, Ashley, my dear sir. This is a great kindness

133

you are showing us,' Bennet boomed, shaking his hand rigorously. He turned to Judith, 'And this is your lady? A thousand thanks, ma'am, and I hope that you and Felicity will become firm friends.' He planted a kiss on the back of Judith's hand, his eyes twinkling at her.

She couldn't help warming to him, and smiled encouragingly at the young woman he drew forward. She was dressed, as was Judith, in plain black, relieved only by a white collar and cuffs, and with a coif covering her mousey brown hair. Judith, still defying Steven, had refused to entirely cover her locks, and caught Felicity's admiring glance. She took heart. Perhaps she could indeed make a close friend of Felicity and enlist her aid. The men would be leaving next morning early and there was no saying when they might be back. Felicity seemed naïve, and Judith determined to woo her over to her side. The idea of using the same methods as Antonia had done caused fission of excitement deep within her. She was missing the enjoyment of mutual physical passion.

Mrs Moffat showed Felicity to their room, and Steven suggested that Judith went along too. He had tactics to discuss with the colonel. There were important matters afoot, and the conflict promised to be harder through the remaining days of summer and autumn. Judith was aware that the chamber to which she accompanied Felicity was the same one that Antonia had occupied. She wondered if Mrs Moffat had done this with the intention of riling her. It was unlikely that Steven would have bothered with such matters, though had shown himself to be malicious.

Felicity glanced around the room that held so many memories for Judith. 'This is very fine,' she exclaimed, followed in by her maid carrying a valise.

'I hope you will be comfortable here.' Judith wanted to say more, but Mrs Moffat was hanging about, all ears. Taking heart in the presence of a guest Judith stared her in the eye and dismissed her. 'You can go now. I will see that Lady Felicity settles in.'

Glad to have scored a point over her Judith became animated as she chatted to her guest, who was like a breath of fresh air blowing through Ferris Mead. She had become used to the company of Antonia's troop and the sense of anticipation that abounded among the Royalists, and found the atmosphere of the manor depressing.

'It's all rather exciting, isn't it?' Felicity babbled as she directed her maid in the unpacking. 'Although I just hate John going into danger and being away for long periods.'

'You love your husband?' Judith watched the vivacious young woman moving about the room.

'Oh, yes. Don't you love and admire yours?' Felicity turned to her, round-eyed.

Judith changed the subject. 'Have you any infants?'

'Not yet, but we are hoping. We've been married three years, and he is such a kind man and looks after our villagers very well. I help to run a school for the children, and if anyone is ill our own doctor attends them. The men were only too willing to fight with him when the call came, but I miss him so much and pray for him constantly. When will this tedious war be over?'

Judith's hope of escaping with Felicity's help faded. She was a loyal supporter of the Parliament, it seemed, or if not fully understanding the principles involved, would follow her husband's lead.

They had supper in the dining room after Steven

had said grace, and it was a pleasant enough occasion. John was loud and jolly and even Steven dropped some of his serious demeanour. Judith found it hard to join in, but Felicity kept up a light chatter, laughing at her husband's jokes and gazing at him adoringly.

When their guests had retired Steven ordered Judith to bed, saying brusquely, 'Get upstairs. I must have a word with Mr Barnes before I join you.'

Judith could not wait to leave him, hoping he might believe her to be asleep when he came to bed. Not that this would make much difference. He would simply demand his rights anyway. She ran up the stairs and came to the door of the guestroom. She could hear the murmur of voices from within. Filled with curiosity she tried to judge how long it would be before Steven finished with Mr Barnes, and if it was possible to creep into the next room and peer through the spy-hole, as she had done with Antonia.

She decided to chance it and let herself in. It was dark, but the moon was shining through the window and she reached the armoire that concealed the aperture in the wall. Screwing up one eye and looking with the other she saw Felicity lying on the bed in the candle-glow. She was naked, her slender body stretched out in complete abandon as she smiled at her husband, who was standing gazing down at her. As bare as he was Judith was granted a full view of his muscular body, and when he turned slightly saw the magnificent spectacle of his cock pointing towards the ceiling, the light glistening on the tear anointing its eye. Beneath this impressive staff hung his balls, swinging as he moved.

Felicity murmured love words and opened herself to him fully, legs spread wide. John lowered himself between them, taking his weight on his arms. He sank down until his face was at her crack, and Judith almost moaned with longing as she saw his tongue penetrating Felicity there, then licking over her swollen bud until she cried out.

'Oh John, John... beloved... I'm coming... oh!'

He gently brought her down from ecstasy and then rolled her over, spread his hands beneath her body and lifted her up towards him, his hard phallus finding the entrance to her vagina. He thrust again and again, his masculine grunts harmonising with Felicity's mewing sounds. He ejaculated in a fierce rush and then they sank down in each other's arms, still kissing and caressing and saying how much they loved one another.

Judith left the room silently, ashamed of having witnessed such an intimate moment between two people who were united in bliss, but sad too, because this wasn't her lot. Steven and she had never known such warmth of feeling, or even liked one another, and now his treatment of her made her actively hate him.

She was more determined than ever to escape from him, harking back to the brief happiness she had known with Antonia and Tom and Mark. Reaching the master chamber she slipped into her night attire and dismissed her maid, and then lay under the quilt, waiting Steven's arrival with trepidation. It was no use feigning sleep for she was wide awake, still picturing the lovers on whom she had just spied.

Her heart sank when he came in, already taking off his garments. Without a word he got into bed, crushing her under his weight and using her as if she was of no more worth than a penny whore. When he freed her at last, turning his back to her and starting to snore, she allowed her imagination free rein as she plotted various ways in which she would like to see him die.

Chapter 8

Felicity was crying as she and Judith waved goodbye to their husbands and the two hundred or so men accompanying them. 'I wish John would let me follow with the other women. He says it would be too hard for me, but I'm sure I could manage,' she sobbed.

They turned back into the house and the staff went about their work. 'He is probably right,' Judith remarked, and then bit her tongue; Felicity mustn't know that she had ridden with an army and seen just how hard the women worked to look after the fighting men.

With Steven's departure she felt as if a great weight had been lifted from her. If she was cunning there might be a chance that she would be gone by the time he returned. But communication was difficult even in peacetime, and the war made it twice as hard. If she could only get a message to Mark, but this was the height of the battle season and when it was over, and the rain and snow set in, roads would be nearly impassable until the spring.

Meanwhile there was Felicity to win over, and Judith took her to the solar, a south-facing room where, for generations, the lady of the manor and her daughters and friends had gathered to work at their embroidery. It was practically a man free area. They had the library, and a gaming room, although this was frowned upon by those of Puritan persuasion.

How did I endure hour after hour of this? she wondered, viewing the canvas stretched on a wooden frame, the many coloured silks in which the design was brought into life, the needles and endless cross-stitch. She said to Felicity as they settled down to sew, 'I was an obedient little girl and this was my only occupation, apart from walks in the garden of my father's house, or a stroll in the long gallery if it was raining.'

Felicity, who by now had dried her eyes and tucked her handkerchief into her sleeve, took her place before her own work, which she had brought with her. 'My life was much the same,' she said. 'Nothing much happened to me until the time came for me to marry John. He owned the estate close to ours and it was an ideal match.'

'Did you love him then?'

'I was flattered that someone so worldly wanted me.' Felicity blushed and stabbed the needle in and out of the painted petals of a flower, bringing it to life. 'He was older, you see, by some ten years, and I looked up to him.'

'And how is he in the marriage bed?' This had to be asked, Judith decided, if they were to make any headway in their friendship, although she already knew the answer after last night's exhibition.

Felicity threw her a startled look. 'This is hardly a subject that should be discussed by ladies.'

Judith had become so accustomed to the frank talk among Antonia and her friends that she had forgotten how prudish many women were. Relationships were whispered about and lovemaking performed in secret. Even when blessed by marriage vows, and no one

139

was supposed to indulge unless this had taken place, coupling was still looked upon as sinful, its main purpose the begetting of children. Pleasure was not supposed to come into it.

The days dragged by and Felicity became more and more agitated because there was no news from John. She opened up to Judith, but not as fully as she had hoped, and it seemed that she was never to free herself from her prison. Steven's absence was a blessing and she slept peacefully without him in the bed. Also, Mrs Moffat's regime relaxed with the master out of the way. As usual she and Mr Barnes robbed the wine cellar and could be heard laughing boisterously at night, and spending much time in each other's bedrooms.

Rumours of the conflict were brought up from the village by the staff, but there was nothing concrete. It seemed as if the opposing forces had reached a stalemate. October was fine and dry, and while the weather lasted so would the battles and sieges. Life at Ferris Mead followed a dull routine and Judith felt she would go mad if she didn't hear from Mark soon. She dreaded to think that he might be dead, but felt that somehow she would know if this happened. It would be as if one half of her no longer existed.

Felicity liked to talk, and under the impression that Judith supported the Parliament was indiscreet about her husband's orders and whereabouts. Judith made a note of everything she said, hoping she might somehow be able to convey it to the Royalists. Although they still occupied separate rooms, Judith became aware that Felicity lingered when it was time to go to sleep.

'I hate going to bed alone,' she complained, her hand on the doorknob. 'I miss John so much.'

It was on the tip of Judith's tongue to ask her to stay, but she wanted the suggestion to come from her. It was not in her nature to be patient, but she was learning this salutary lesson, gritting her teeth and waiting. Her behaviour was exemplary and she gave Mrs Moffat no cause to be suspicious.

It seemed that autumn had arrived at last when, one evening after they had retired, rain started to fall in torrents, lighting flashed and thunder rumbled overhead. Judith's first thoughts as she lay listening to it were, oh God, this means the end of campaigning. Steven will be returning soon. I shall have to endure the winter with him in the house. No chance of escaping when snow is thick on the ground.

There was a timid knock on the door and Felicity saying in a trembling voice, 'Are you awake, Judith? I'm so afraid of thunder.'

Now was the moment. Judith lifted the bedclothes and patted the space beside her. 'Come and join me,' she said.

Without any hesitation Felicity climbed in beside her. Judith slipped an arm around her and cuddled her close, stilling her fears. She had grown fond of Felicity over the time they'd spent together, feeling towards her like the younger sister she had never had, or the baby she had not yet conceived. It was a warm, loving feeling.

It was weeks since she had been to bed to someone she liked, and she pushed from her mind the thought of Steven. Sleeping with him drained her and damaged her soul. Then she realised that Felicity was straining to get nearer, and her own frustrated passions stirred. Antonia had awakened her slumbering senses and Tom and Mark had done the

141

rest. She missed physical contact. Perhaps Felicity felt the same.

'Do you long to feel John in your arms?' she asked softly.

'Oh, yes,' Felicity sighed, the warmth of her breasts penetrating her cambric nightgown, and Judith's too. 'He gives me pleasure I never dreamed existed, although I had discovered how to play with myself. I've taken to doing so whenever he's away, but it isn't the same. Do you do this?'

Her artless words were fuelling Judith's fire and she allowed her hands to move over Felicity's breasts, feeling the nipples crimp in response. 'Yes,' she whispered. 'But I must confess that Steven is not a considerate lover. Might I suggest that we console one another, you for John's absence, and I for my husband's lack of understanding of my needs?'

'How do you mean?' Felicity asked, although she was instinctively moving her hips and pressing against Judith's thigh.

'I could make love to you and you to me. Women sometimes do this, and often prefer it to men.' While Judith talked she unfastened the pearl buttons that fastened Felicity's night attire. She slipped a hand inside and encountered her soft warm flesh, hearing her gasp in response.

Felicity lifted her hips from the mattress as Judith worked her way down, her middle finger finally encountering the sliver of flesh between her sex lips, now moist and swollen. Judith increased that enticing friction, bending to suck one of Felicity's nipples. 'Go on, don't stop,' she cried, her pubis pressed against Judith's seductive movements.

Using all the technique she had acquired under Antonia's tutelage Judith brought her closer and closer to bliss, until at last she heard her scream in ecstasy and felt her sink back, satiated. By now her own passions were fully aroused and she dipped down to feel between her legs where she was wet with love juice. She gently spread it over her clitoris, which was aching with need.

Felicity propped herself up on one elbow and shyly asked, 'Would you mind if I did the same to you? I've never touched a woman intimately.'

'Oh, please do, I need to be satisfied,' Judith said eagerly, and immediately felt those untried fingers creeping across her belly and through her pubic hair. She was hesitant and shy, but gained confidence as Judith gasped, 'That's wonderful. Go on with what you're doing.' There was extra excitement in training a novice, and she realised that this is what Antonia must have experienced when she introduced her to female loving.

'Do you like it?' Felicity's voice shook. 'What a soft part of you. So different to a man's hard rod.'

'And far more sensitive, so it seems.' Judith's thighs were slack and her knees fallen apart to expose herself as Felicity bent over her. 'I'd like you to kiss me there.'

'Ah yes, John does that to me sometimes and I, in turn, suck his manhood.' Felicity lowered her head and Judith felt her lips exploring her groin, and then holding back her labia and applying her tongue to the tip of her pleasure organ.

Judith could not restrain her cries and she clasped Felicity's head, holding her to the spot that was the female mount of pleasure. Her tongue fondled it, while Judith stretched her labia apart so that her nubbin protruded. She could feel it pulsating and thrills ran up her spine, the sensation mounting and mounting until she exploded into a mighty orgasm. Felicity seemed to know instinctively when it was over.

They held each other close and were almost asleep when Judith said, 'The storm is over, my dear. You must return to your own bed, lest Mrs Moffat or one of the servants finds us like this in the morning.'

'Very well.' Felicity climbed out of bed. 'But may we do this again?'

'Oh yes,' Judith answered, for not only was it extremely pleasant, but the fonder Felicity became the more likely she was to help her.

The weather brightened, and two days later Mrs Moffat came to the solar and said, 'There's a peddler at the side-door, my lady. Are you in need of sewing silks or the like?'

Judith looked up, but Felicity was already on her feet. 'A peddler? How exciting! He is sure to have interesting things for sale.'

These itinerants travelled from village to village or manor house to manor house, supplying goods that could not otherwise be purchased except for a visit to one of the big towns, and this was a rare occurrence. Places like Ferris Mead produced everything for daily needs. There was a dairy, a bakery, a butchery, and a laundry. Orchards provided fruit, vegetables grew in the garden and corn in the fields, and livestock were maintained in lush pastures. The villagers also supplied themselves from their own plots of land, so the arrival of a peddler was quite an event.

Judith led Felicity to where he stood, under the watchful eye of Mr Barnes. Several servants were already gathered around, but they parted to let the ladies through. 'This is Lady Ashwell, fellow,' Mr

Barnes said sternly. 'Accord her the greatest servility.'

The peddler bowed low, his voice gruff as he muttered, 'Your servant, madam.'

He was grizzled and bowed, his clothing patched and worn, and he carried his pack on a strap around his neck, the lid back displaying his wares. Through the open door Judith could see a small canvas-covered cart, harnessed to an elderly-looking nag. Any diversion was welcome to relieve the boredom. 'Let me see what you have on offer,' she said, smiling at him and moving closer.

He held out his pack and she picked out a tortoiseshell comb, a hand-mirror and a pair of white kid gloves. While she was handing him money to pay for these he slipped something into her palm. It was a square of folded paper and she quickly concealed it. She looked into his face and he dropped an eyelid in a wink. She suddenly saw that he was younger than he seemed. With a rapidly beating heart she waited impatiently for Felicity to make her purchases and the peddler to leave.

When alone in her room she opened the note and read. 'Beloved, be at the crossroad near Marsh Way at noon tomorrow. Take your coach as if going to visit the church. Mark.'

She could hardly believe it, reading it over and over. He said no more than this and she guessed that the peddler was one of his associates. But how could she possibly do this? She was almost as much of a prisoner as Antonia had been. Then she decided to assert her authority and called for Mrs Moffat, and when the woman came in she smelled strongly of drink and this was all to the good.

'Mrs Moffat, I wish you to order the coach to be

ready in the morning. Lady Felicity has expressed the desire to visit the church, and as my guest, it is my duty to please her.'

'But my lady…' Mrs Moffat began unsteadily, but Judith silenced her.

'Do as I say. I shall go to Lady Felicity now and tell her.'

'Very well, my lady, but I shall chaperone you both.' Mrs Moffat left the room in a hurry. No doubt she wanted to get back to the wine cellar.

Judith went to see Felicity, who was delighted at the idea of an outing. She hinted that she would like to share Judith's bed that night, but she had too much on her mind, needing her own company to speculate as to what the note implied. Could it be Antonia arranging to rescue her? Or maybe Mark? She was too excited to sleep and was up at the crack of dawn, preparing herself, although not betraying herself to Mrs Moffat who arrived around eleven, dressed ready for the outing. Felicity's maid was to come as well, and the coach waited, along with two grooms standing at the back.

Afterwards Judith never remembered how she maintained her calm. Not only was she embarking on another adventure, but this was the first time she had been further than the garden since Steven captured her. It was a dull morning but dry, and the coach lumbered down the uneven road that led towards the church. Her heart was thudding as they neared the crossroads, and there the carriage lurched to a sudden halt, Judith peering from the window to see a masked man training a pistol on the coachman.

'Halt!' he cried as four others appeared, their faces covered and hats pulled down low. The grooms were also at pistol-point. 'The occupants are to get out and hand all their valuables over to me,' the leader commanded.

'Oh, mercy me!' Mrs Moffat was close to hysterics. 'We're all to be killed! These are highway robbers!'

Felicity was comforting her terrified maid as they all obeyed the masked man. He was still mounted but a couple of his men were going round on foot, taking anything of value. The coachman and grooms were of no help, standing there trembling in fear for their lives.

It was all over very quickly, the men on their horses again and then their leader said, 'Get back into the coach now, but don't attempt to raise the alarm until we are well on our way.' As Judith turned to obey he reached down and grabbed her. 'Not you, lady! You are to come with me as a hostage. No doubt your husband will pay handsomely for a beauty like you.'

Before she could protest he swung her up before him, dug his heels into his mount's sides and was away, his men thundering after him. Judith was neither alarmed nor horrified. Although the highwayman was masked she could tell who it was that held her so tightly, and joy filled her whole being. It was Mark.

It grew dark early now, and after putting many miles between them and Ferris Mead Mark and his men cantered into the yard of an inn whose landlord was friendly to their cause. Judith slid from the saddle into his arms and he pulled off the scarf that hid his face and grinned down at her. 'Oh, Mark,' she cried, 'is it really you?'

'It better be,' he joked. 'I don't want you spending the night with a highway robber.'

147

She had never been happier; all the lifeblood that had been dammed within her while a captive to her husband came flooding back. In a daze she sat with him and his companions while they ate in the bar parlour.

'How did you succeed in doing this?' she asked, in wonder.

He held her hand and included the others in the tale. 'The Prince could not spare men to attack Ferris Mead, but at last allowed me to get you if I could. For some time now Cavaliers have been setting out on their own, becoming the leaders of a group of stout-hearted fellows and attacking Parliamentarian coaches, robbing them and giving the money to the Royalist cause. I decided to do the same to get you out of your husband's clutches, and it worked well. You are here, and you are free.'

She smiled around the table at all of them. 'Thank you, thank you.'

'Now we're returning to Oxford. The weather is on the turn but we shall follow the Prince's orders and do what we can to harass the Roundheads.'

'And Antonia and Frankie and Tom?'

'They are well and waiting to see you, but I must tell you that the Roundheads grow ever stronger under Cromwell, who is training his men and calling them the Ironsides. The future looks bleak, but never mind that now. Let us drink to His Majesty, and then retire.'

Glasses were raised and then accommodation was found for the weary riders. Mark spoke to the landlord and he lit them to a double room, and set a taper to the logs in the wide hearth. Mark took Judith's hands in his. 'You are freezing. Let me warm you.' He drew her to the fire.

'The cold is nothing; I am so happy,' she murmured, resting back against him. 'I thought I would never see you again.' She recounted everything that had happened since she was imprisoned by Steven, and Mark's face darkened as he listened and held her and kissed her gently.

'Your husband is a monster,' he muttered. 'I would like to challenge him to a duel and fight for you, beloved.'

She clung to him. 'You must be careful. He is a vengeful man and I couldn't bear to lose you again. I have asked him to annul the marriage, but he refuses.'

'Come to bed, dear heart, and I will warm you properly,' he said, and within minutes they were under the quilt, naked as the day they were born.

It was so familiar, but strange too, and Judith could not quite believe it. Making love with Felicity had been enjoyable, and Judith sincere in her liking for the girl, but to lie with Mark was her wildest dream come true. She revelled in the feel of his flesh next to hers, his chest coated with a sprinkling of hair, his arms and legs too, the masculine smell of him and the way he had of caressing her and bringing her to orgasm. And then the magical moment when he took possession of her body, not harshly like Steven, but with the greatest passion and tenderness.

But once was not enough, and after they had rested a little he began to stroke her again, finding the pleasure bud and adding to its sensitivity by attention to her nipples too. She in turn kissed his cock, holding back the foreskin and sucking his helm as if it was the most delectable of sweetmeats, and finally receiving his libation in her mouth. The hours passed and still they wanted more, their separation adding to their need for one another.

Judith had never before given herself so openly, neither to man or woman. She did not want to be parted from this person, whom she was sure was her soul-mate. She pushed the war from her mind. For the rest of the night Mark was hers and she was his. Who could tell what might happen tomorrow?

Chapter 9

'You are back in the land of the living, thank God!' enthused Antonia, when she walked into Isobel's house and saw Judith. More delighted than she had thought possible she clasped her in a tight embrace, then held her off and studied her face. 'I can see you've been through a bad time.'

'Mark rescued me,' Judith exclaimed, and tears filled her eyes. 'You can have no notion how glad I am to be here.'

Antonia took off her hat, her baldric and sword, and loosened her shirt collar and doublet. She was concerned about Judith, who was pale and drawn and nervous, clinging to Mark's hand. She listened to the account of her captivity and wished she could lay hands on Steven Ashley, but this was unlikely for the armies of both sides had ceased fire for the winter. Oxford was no longer a centre of optimism and many were leaving for abroad. The Royalists troops had taken a battering lately, and the outcome of victory for the king was no longer certain.

'Where is Prince Rupert?' Mark asked, seated by Judith. They both looked scruffy and tired.

'All over the place, as usual. He dashes from city to city that are still for His Majesty, raising troops, stirring up enthusiasm, though it is getting increasingly difficult. I'm not at all sure how long Oxford can hold out. Isobel is talking about heading for Paris, where she has money and property.'

'Indeed I am,' volunteered Isobel, catching the end of the conversation as she came in. 'Soon it won't be safe here. We should get out while we still can.'

'We can't abandon the cause,' Antonia said, although she was hearing similar sentiments on every side these days. 'What about the king? If he falls into the hands of his enemies it could be very bad for him.'

'Can't he and the Parliament come to some kind of compromise?' suggested Mark.

Antonia shrugged. 'Who knows? Rupert is in disgrace, his uncle blaming him for the recent defeats.'

Isobel sighed and moved restlessly. 'Everyone is so gloomy these days; I really can't be doing with it. Nearly all the best people have left, and there are no balls and soirées being held any more. It is positively dull.'

'War isn't meant to be entertaining, especially civil war,' Mark reprimanded.

'Oh, come now! You must admit that it was exhilarating in the beginning, when we thought it would be all over in a few months and the king back on his throne in Whitehall Palace.'

Antonia listened to Isobel's complaints and agreed that many people were thinking the same. She had no plan of action for herself, but would stay faithful to Rupert and fight with him and for him as long as she was able. Jamie was in his company at the moment, somewhere in the Midlands, and now Antonia felt the need to relax. Isobel's flippant attitude might be annoying, but she was such a beautiful creature and offered bountiful delights of the flesh. Winter was the time for rest and recuperation, and Antonia determined to stop worrying and enjoy it.

'You need to recover after your ordeal,' she said to Judith and Mark. 'Go back to headquarters. Sergeant Miller will let you in, and you can stay in the house. I shall remain here for a while. I'll see you tomorrow and we can talk further.'

'I have some information for you,' Judith replied. 'Colonel Bennet's lady, Felicity, was staying with me at Ferris Mead while he and Steven were off fighting, and we became friends. She was careless in her talk, and I noted down what she let slip concerning Roundhead movements.'

'Good. Let me have all you know and it may prove of help.' Antonia poured herself a glass of wine and saw them out, then turned to Isobel. 'Shall we retire to your chamber, or are you expecting another lover?'

'I'm not and was contemplating a lonely night.' Isobel wound her arms around Antonia's neck. 'You are still my favourite soldier. It will be a shame when hostilities are over and you have to revert to women's clothes again.'

Antonia ran her tongue around Isobel's lobe, setting the earring swinging. 'Who says that I shall? I can't see Rupert giving up, can you? He talks of going to sea, becoming a pirate and harassing Roundhead shipping. I might go with him.'

Isobel stiffened, saying crossly, 'Are you still hankering after him? You know that it's useless. If he ever settles down, which I doubt, then he'll have to marry a royal princess.'

Antonia shrugged it off. 'What makes you think I want him? I simply admire his military skill, that's all.'

'And the rest,' Isobel teased. 'You never have told me how big he is. Does his cock match his size and girth?'

That is one of Isobel's faults, Antonia thought, as they retired to the bedchamber. She does like to know intimate details. 'I'm not prepared to discuss it,' she said huffily.

Isobel's laughter rang through the room. 'In that case I'll assume that it's no bigger than my little finger.' She waggled it in front of Antonia's face. 'I've often found that big men don't necessarily have big pricks, whereas the tackle of smaller men can be surprising.'

To stop her chatter Antonia kissed her full on the lips, which parted and her agile tongue sampled her lover's mouth. Then Isobel withdrew enough to say, 'I've missed you. I never know where you are from one day to the next.'

'I'm a soldier. I have to obey my commander's orders.'

'Well I am your commander at this moment, and you will do as I say.'

Antonia entered into the spirit of it. 'Of course, Your Mightiness. What would you have me do?'

'Undress, for a start.' Isobel was already divesting herself, slowly and provocatively, baring her body as only she knew how. It would have taken a saint to resist her.

Antonia followed her example, first her shirt, leaving her naked to the waist, and then sitting to tug at her boots and remove her stockings. Last of all she unlaced her breeches, letting them drop, followed by

153

the white undergarment worn beneath.

The firelight bathed them in a golden glow, and Antonia reached out for Isobel and they stood together before the flames, enjoying the warmth and the sensation of flesh against flesh. Antonia forgot the war and Judith and even ceased to dwell on Rupert.

'You still have a scar.' Isobel ran a finger along the injury sustained when Steven had captured Antonia.

'It will always remain,' she replied. 'I have been lucky so far, and it was a blessing in disguise for it helped me to free Judith from a tyrannical husband.'

'You're fond of her?'

'She is brave and trustworthy, and there are few I can say that about.' Antonia climbed into bed, and Isobel followed.

It was warm and safe there, and they lay in the semi-darkness talking and caressing until gradually their speech became halting as passion took over. They knew each other well, and what they needed to reach orgasm. The intensity of their feelings surpassed that experienced with men, although Antonia's love for Rupert amounted to adoration. She modelled herself on him when acting the soldier, and became feminine when he needed physical satisfaction. In Isobel's embrace she could mimic the roughness of the male, or melt into submission as a woman. All these various aspects added to the glorious games they could play together.

'I've missed you,' Isobel pouted. 'What kept you away so long?'

'I have to follow orders and took part in several skirmishes, but now I am here with you, my amorous mistress.' Antonia assumed the role of a soldier, and Isobel responded.

This was a role Antonia loved acting out. The army life fulfilled her. Although she was aware that if she lived through all this she might have to resume her position as a landowner and find a husband and produce an heir, just for now she was enjoying the present.

'Oh yes, take me,' Isobel mewed. 'I want…'

'I know what you want.' Antonia knelt over her, the palms of her hands laid on each of her thighs, parting them so that her secrets were exposed.

Isobel reached up and cupped Antonia's breasts, her thumbs rolling each nipple. Antonia lowered her head and licked Isobel's wet cleft. Then she reached for the wine glass, dipped her fingers into it and trickled red drops over the swollen, needy bud, and tongued it. Isobel's whimpers turned into shrill cries and Antonia felt her spasm as she reached a climax. She could smell the oceanic fragrance of her own juices mingled with her lover's, and needed completion.

Isobel opened her eyes and looked up at her. 'Now I shall pleasure you,' she promised.

When Judith woke next morning she could hardly believe she was in Oxford. Mark was moving about the room, preparing to leave and fully armed. She sat up abruptly. 'Where are you going?'

He came across to the bed. 'Sweetheart, I have to join those reconnoitring the city so the farmers can drive in with their goods to keep Oxford fed. The Roundheads try to prevent this, hoping to starve us out.'

'Why can't I come?' She hated to have him out of her sight for a moment. They'd slept together and it had been heavenly, but now it seemed she was to lose

155

him again.

'Sergeant Miller gave me my orders last night. He thought it would be wise for you to rest for a day or two. Don't worry, I'll be back.' He leaned over and kissed her, then freed himself from her arms and went out of the door.

Unable to stay still Judith dressed in the plain gown she'd worn when she left Ferris Mead, and made her way down to find breakfast and Sergeant Miller, in that order. 'You're not fit to fight yet,' he said stubbornly. 'I've heard what happened to you at Marston Moor, and think it unwise to involve you.'

'But I can't sit around here doing nothing,' she protested.

'There's not much taking place while the weather's bad, as you already know. Only a few of our lads keeping an eye on the whereabouts of the enemy. You'll have enough fighting come the spring, so I advise you to make the most of this.'

In a temper Judith walked to where Isobel lived and found Antonia in her bedroom, tucking into a hearty meal. 'I'm not allowed to take up arms again,' she complained.

'Not yet,' Antonia confirmed, a piece of bacon balanced on her knife. 'Stop fretting your bowels to fiddle strings.'

'I want my husband dead!' Judith took a chair beside her and held out her hands to the flames.

'I should think you're not alone in this desire; no doubt many wives feel the same,' Antonia joked.

'Don't make fun of her,' Isobel scolded.

'I mean it,' Judith shouted.

'I don't think we can do a lot at the present.' Antonia was trying to calm her. 'No doubt he'll be holed up in your house by now.'

'And giving the servants hell because I have escaped again, and I can take some comfort in this.' Judith visualised Mrs Moffat being the brunt of Steven's wrath.

Isobel was wearing a silk negligee and sitting before the mirror, combing out her mane of chestnut curls. She looked as smug as a cat that has been at the cream. She cast a glance at Judith. 'I am thinking of leaving for France soon, if things don't brighten up here.'

Judith was shocked. 'Do you really mean you will abandon the cause?'

'What else can I do? I have a house in Paris and money in the bank there. Why don't you come with me?'

'I wouldn't feel it to be right. Besides, what about Mark? I'm sure he will fight as long as he is able. Will you go, Antonia?'

'I have no plans to do so. Who knows, the war may swing in our favour once hostilities are resumed.'

'There you are then, Isobel. There's your answer. I shall stay, and I would be grateful if you could help me purchase doublets and breeches again.'

Isobel softened, smiling. 'Very well, you mad hot-headed wench, but the offer is there should you want to take it. Meanwhile, off with that dreadful dress. I have prettier gowns that will fit you.'

When Steven and John walked into Ferris Mead the servants had already given a garbled version of Judith's abduction. He reached the great hall where Mrs Moffat and Mr Barnes waited, both pale and agitated.

'What has been happening here, and where is Lady Ashley?' he demanded, in an impossible position for

157

he did not want John Bennet to know about his wife's former transgressions, and had a strong suspicion that this was another episode organised by her and her Royalist friends.

'We were held up by highway robbers,' Mrs Moffat faltered, wringing her hands together. 'I was with her, my lord, and so were Lady Felicity and her maid.'

'Why had they left the house?' He scowled at her blackly.

'Lady Felicity expressed the desire to visit the church, sir. I thought there would be no harm for them to have a trip out while the weather was fine. Please, my lord, don't blame me. I was only doing what I thought was right.'

Felicity ran into her husband's arms, sobbing. 'Oh John, it was terrible! I was so frightened. There were a gang of horsemen, you see, and their leader commanded us to hand over our valuables. They took my wedding ring! We thought that was all, and then he ordered Judith to go with him saying he was holding her to ransom, and that Steven would pay to get her back.'

'Hush, darling,' John soothed. 'It's all right; I'm here now.'

'Is this true, Mrs Moffat?' Steven was deeply suspicious.

'Yes sir, every word of it,' she sniffed, handkerchief to her eyes.

'And has a ransom demand arrived?'

'Not that I am aware, sir.'

He turned his anger on Mr Barnes. 'Well, fellow, have you seen any such message?'

'No, my lord.'

'Tsha! You both reek of wine. Been at my cellar

again, have you, instead of doing you duty? Away with you, I need to discuss this with Colonel Bennet.'

Everything within him said that this was an arranged kidnapping, and he longed to get his hands on the perpetrators. He'd drag information out of anyone involved, by torture if necessary, and the thought of doing this made his groin ache. He needed to question the servants and whip a confession out of one of them, but could do nothing until John and Felicity had departed.

They did so almost at once, eager to get home to their cosy domesticity, and Steven stood at the top of the front steps watching them leave, with Felicity and her maid in one coach while John rode alongside, and another holding baggage and half a dozen servants and his soldiers marching behind. Steven switched off his false smile and ordered Mr Barnes to assemble all the staff in the great hall.

They gathered, indoor and outdoor workers, all murmuring among themselves and casting apprehensive glances at Mrs Moffat and Mr Barnes. They dared not even look at their master, who was renowned for his temper. He stood facing them, two steps up on the grand staircase, the extra height making him even more threatening. He held up a hand for silence.

'As you all know Lady Ashley has been kidnapped… supposedly. I want you to say if you saw anything unusual around that time. Did strangers call at the house? Speak out.'

One of the recently employed maids raised her arm. She was a bold girl, no doubt hoping to curry favour with the master. 'Please, sir… your lordship. I did see a peddler who came to the door the day before milady was snatched.'

'A peddler?' Steven roared, turning on Mrs Moffat. 'You didn't tell me about this, woman!'

'Mr Barnes was in charge.'

'You were present too,' Barnes cried indignantly.

'Did the ladies see him and purchase anything?' Steven's suspicions became a certainty.

'They did, sir, I saw them,' piped up the maid, happy to be the centre of attention. 'Lady Ashley spoke to him and bought a few bits and pieces.'

'Is that all? They didn't converse?' Steven's rage was getting out of control. 'If I find out that this was a plot and you a part of it then you'll regret it bitterly!'

The girl's pertness disappeared and she cringed. 'I swear to you, my lord, I don't know nothing about it. I'd never set eyes on him before.'

The rest of them began to mutter, denying all knowledge of the peddler, but someone had to suffer and Steven's fury descended on Mrs Moffat. He thrust an accusing finger at her, shouting, 'You neglected your duty. I'm sure this wench knows more than she is saying. Get her to the punishment room. You shall be present and we'll find out exactly how much she is involved in this plot, if plot it be.'

Mrs Moffat leapt to attention, giving the girl a shove in the back. 'Come along, Polly, you heard what his lordship said.' Between them she and Mr Barnes frogmarched the protesting girl away.

Steven followed more slowly after dismissing the staff to go back to their duties. All of them were silent and cowed and this gave him great satisfaction, as it did when his soldiers obeyed his commands. It gave him a dizzying sense of power. He walked along a corridor and down a flight of steps that led to the room where punishment for misdemeanours was meted out.

It was a gloomy place, close to the dungeon where Judith had been imprisoned. Mr Barnes lit the candles and then departed with orders to see that the others went about their tasks.

'Let me go, sir,' Polly begged. 'I ain't done nothing, I promise. Tell him, Mrs Moffat.'

The housekeeper raised her cane and Polly cringed. 'Be quiet, girl! How dare you gainsay our lord and master? He knows what's right or wrong.'

Polly ran towards the door but Steven barred her way, squeezing her arm hard. 'And where do you think you're going?' His voice was charged with menace. 'I want some answers out of you. Did you know the peddler?'

Polly shook her head, tears coursing down her cheeks. 'No sir, I didn't.'

Steven nodded to Mrs Moffat, who leapt forward and helped him drag the struggling girl to the wall, where iron rings hung, complete with manacles. Polly was pushed face against the bricks, her arms raised above her head and cuffs clamped around her wrists. 'Strip her,' he ordered.

Polly yelled in protest but Mrs Moffat yanked at her clothing, although hampered by her tethered arms. 'Shall I tear her garments?' she ventured, unable to conceal the smile that twisted her face.

'Do what is necessary.' Steven could feel his cock thickening, and sensed that the housekeeper was gaining pleasure from this too. For some time he had suspected that she had unnatural desires, but his Puritan upbringing had not permitted him to dwell on it, in the same way that he tried to suppress his own lustful longings.

He liked the sight as the back of Polly's simple

161

dress was unlaced and opened, exposing her chemise. It was ripped, her spine exposed to her buttocks and beyond. The skirt and petticoat fell away and he could see the tops of her black woollen stockings, upheld by plain garters. The sight of the deep divide between her thighs caused his penis to rise uncomfortably within his breeches. He yearned to plunge it between those milky white hillocks, but first they must be marked with scarlet from his whip, which would increase his passion and insure a mighty outpouring of his semen.

'She is ready, sir,' Mrs Moffat pronounced breathlessly.

They both feasted their eyes on the helpless, naked, manacled girl. Steven was almost sure that she had told the truth, but someone had to pay for Judith's escape and Polly was an ideal candidate. To his everlasting shame he desired women who were not of his class. He had been suckled by a wet nurse, as was the custom among the gentry, and had never been close to his mother. His nurses had provided glimpses of the female form and he'd listened to their careless chatter. In his early teens one of them took him into her bed and taught him about sex, although not showing him how to satisfy a woman. He was torn between fleshy desires and a strict religious upbringing, so something twisted within him wanted to punish women and at that moment Polly provided an ideal opportunity, although he wished it was Judith.

'Come now, girl,' he growled. 'Confess that you knew the peddler and were party to the plot.'

'No sir, I swear it on my mother's life!' Polly cried. 'Let me go and I'll leave your service and trouble you no more.'

This was the moment for which Steven had been waiting. The whip in his hand felt like an extension of his arm. He raised it and the crack it made as it contacted her flesh was music to his ears. So was Polly's agonised yell. He heard Mrs Moffat's gasp and saw her eyes glinting as she leaned closer. He no longer cared if Polly was guilty or not. The whip slashed at her again, and she was screaming in earnest.

'What do you want me to say?' she wailed desperately. 'I'll do anything if you'll only stop!'

The whip bit into her again. 'Did you see her speak to him?' Steven snarled.

'No sir! Oh, please stop! Wait, wait… I might have seen him pass something to her when she put coins in his hand.'

'A note?' Steven flexed the whip.

'Perhaps, I'm not sure. I weren't paying much attention.'

'I knew it!' Steven muttered, his worst fears confirmed. 'They got in contact with her, those godless Cavaliers, and she took advantage of it. Held to ransom? A lie! She has run off with them again!'

'Can I go now, my lord?' Polly whimpered.

'I think you deserve another stroke for holding this information back. What do you say, Mrs Moffat?'

'Oh yes, at least one, sir,' she answered eagerly.

Steven braced himself and raised his arm. Polly quivered, awaiting the stroke. He let her wait, and then brought down the lash with full force and she screamed and pleaded through her sobs. 'No more, my lord! I'll do anything, anything, but don't whip me again!'

The temptation to take her was almost too much for him. He thrust the whip into Mrs Moffat's hand and left abruptly, standing outside the door, breeches undone while he watched her beat the girl and then finger her intimately. He clutched his cock and came into his hand, after which he gave the housekeeper orders to free Polly and took himself off to his room, there to brood on how he was to get Judith back.

Chapter 10

The winter was harsh and relentless, but Judith wished it would go on for ever. Mark was with her more often than not, and she loved being in the warmth of his arms within their bed while the snow fell heavily outside Antonia's headquarters. She was not interested in the society life beloved by Isobel, who was doing her best to keep it going. Oxford had settled down into an acceptance of the bad weather, though the Royalist leaders were already planning their campaign, which would start as soon as the roads were clear.

She saw Antonia often, and was glad to unburden herself to someone who knew Steven.

'And if he were to die Ferris Mead would come to you, as his widow?' Antonia asked. 'There is no one else who would inherit?'

'I don't know. His nephew, Nicolas, perhaps. But don't forget that Steven is a Parliamentarian, and they are unlikely to sign it over to me, as I have joined the other side.'

'When the war is won and the king back on his throne those who fought against him will be deprived of their properties, and those who supported him will be rewarded,' Antonia said, with more conviction than she felt.

'I want to fight again,' Judith declared.

'I know you do, and soon Sergeant Miller will have you out there on the parade ground, along with the others, putting you through your paces in case you have grown soft during the respite.'

'I can't wait! Is there no chance we can attack Ferris Mead and kill Steven?'

'Leave it to me. I have a plan.'

'Can I be a part of it?'

Antonia kissed her cheek, ready to go. 'I will let you know.'

'Promise me that you won't go after him without taking me. I would like to see him humiliated.' Sometimes Judith's hatred startled even herself, but she could not find it in her heart to forgive him.

Judith's vehemence did not surprise Antonia, and she agreed that she had every right to feel so strongly. For her own part she had a score to settle with him. His treatment of her had displayed what sort of a man he was, and she would have challenged him then and there had she been able.

Christmas had come and gone and the weather was improving, though not enough to engage in major encounters. Antonia, Mark and Tom met up and planned what they were going to do about Judith's husband. He had to be taught a lesson at least, and both she and Mark longed to engage him in a duel. Tom was more than just useful as he knew the area well, and also the running of the Ferris Mead household, including the master's movements and routine.

'Wait,' Mark advised, seated with them in the Rose

165

and Crown tavern, where he had lodged at one time. It had sentimental associations for him, as it was where he and Judith had first consummated their love. It was a favourite drinking place for the soldiers. 'I understand we'll be marching that way soon, in order to attack a Roundhead stronghold.'

'I know this. Rupert told me. That is why I am planning to somehow meet up with Steven Ashley and give him the trouncing he deserves.'

'Let me challenge him. Judith will never be free while he's alive. He has refused to have the marriage annulled. If he is dead she may inherit as his widow, once the war is over.'

'And if it doesn't go in our favour?'

Mark looked uneasily into his tankard of beer. 'We'll face that if and when it happens. Meanwhile, is Judith to fight alongside of us?'

'Not this time. I am her commanding officer and will help her to see the sense of travelling in the baggage wagons with the other women, until she has recovered from her last ordeal.' Antonia was determined on this course.

'She won't like it,' Tom warned, then added proudly, 'although my girl will be with her. We're getting married tomorrow. Lady Judith knows all about it and is happy for us.'

Although it was true that Judith had congratulated the pair she was rebellious about becoming a camp follower, though agreed that she had lost her nerve at the major battle during which she'd been captured. The women did an important job, keeping up morale and caring for the sick and injured. The major bonus was that Mark would be in Antonia's regiment, and they would be able to meet. So she made a friend of Emma, Tom's bride, donned a plain dress and wrapped a shawl around her shoulders, ready to join the fray in a different capacity.

Holt Hall was some distance away, a Roundhead stronghold in the same county as Ferris Mead. Taking it would give the Royalists access to a bridge across the river. Judith was apprehensive about meeting up with Steven, who would no doubt be helping in its defence.

After a day's journey they pitched camp, male and she-soldiers resting, and the women attending to their needs. Judith slipped around to the back of the wagon she was sharing with several others and fell into Mark's arms.

'Oh darling,' she murmured. 'I'm so glad to be with you, but I wish so much that I could fight by your side tomorrow. How can I bear to be in the background while you face danger?'

'Never fear, sweetheart. I shall return to you.' It was chilly and he wrapped his cloak around them both, and drew her into the shelter of a copse. There he pressed her back against a tree, his arms hemming her in as he kissed her face and ears, her neck and throat, and then feasted on her mouth. She parted her lips for his invasion. It was growing dark but she feared nothing if he was with her. She caressed his face, tracing his features with her fingers and inhaling the scent of his long curls. He unbuttoned her bodice, baring her breasts to his touch.

'Dear God, I want you so much,' he whispered, and eased off his sword belt, letting the weapon fall to the ground. Then he lifted her, skirts falling back as she straddled his waist and hung there, gripping him around his neck.

Holding her with one arm he unlaced his breeches and she felt the harness of his cock pressing against

167

her. She lowered a hand and guided him into her damp love channel, then slid a finger to her clitoris and massaged it as he thrust in and out. Her position allowed the deepest penetration, his helm jutting against her womb as she came to a climax. Arms about him again she clung there, sighing and sighing as he too reached his apogee.

'Oh Mark, will there ever be a time when we can be together for ever?'

He lowered her to her feet and fastened up. 'I pray for this, sweeting. Judith, will you marry me once you are free from your husband?'

There was nothing she could say but, 'Yes! Oh yes!'

He then walked her back to the circle of wagons and there, in the firelight glow, she glimpsed Tom and Emma locked in an embrace, and envied them because they had already made their marriage vows.

To remain behind while the men rode off to attack Holt Hall was the hardest thing Judith had ever done. She could only marvel at the courage and fortitude of the other women who had travelled like this for months, never knowing if their men were to be brought back from battle dead or seriously injured.

'All we can do is pray, my dear,' said one, stout and genial and a fount of good advice. 'At least I shall know that I stood by my Peter until the last.'

Such fortitude made Judith ashamed and she joined Emma in the long wait, hoping that Holt Hall would surrender soon and a messenger arrive with the good news. They were guarded by soldiers, ordered to beat off the enemy should they attempt to steal provisions from the leaguer.

Antonia was in the forefront. Holt Hall had been stubborn for months and the Royalists needed to take it. Other troops had arrived earlier bringing cannon with them, and were preparing to blast the walls. Meanwhile Rupert had ridden close, shouting to those on the ramparts to surrender without further ado, and all within would be spared. But they remained defiant, shots ringing out as he turned his horse and rejoined the ranks. He gave the artillery orders to fire. The blast was earth-shattering and a large hole appeared in one of the main walls. A cheer arose from the attackers and, banners waving, they prepared to advance.

Antonia was among the lead, seeking one man only. She climbed in through the hole and found herself in a courtyard, attacked on all sides by the defenders. She beat them off, and aware that Tom and Mark were behind her ran into the great hall. Rupert was already there, sword in hand, like a whirlwind striking down any who stood in his way. His men were behind him thrusting and slashing, and it seemed that the defenders were about to surrender. Suddenly she saw Steven amidst the turmoil. He was fighting grimly.

'There he is!' she shouted over her shoulder to Mark, and in that fraught moment Steven saw and recognised her. He backed out of the hall into a side-room, two of his men with him. Antonia gave chase, with Mark and Tom in her wake.

'You!' Steven shouted, lunging at her. 'You devil woman who corrupted my wife!' Antonia parried his blow, aware of nothing but that her enemy was before her and she had the chance to best him. She lunged but he stepped back, and then flourished his blade. Mark and Tom were holding off those who tried to come to Steven's aid, but, 'Stand back!' he roared. 'This is between her and me!'

She could tell he was a skilled swordsman, but his temperament gave him a disadvantage. He was too aggressive. Steel rang on steel as their weapons met then broke free. She went forward but he feinted, avoiding the blow and attacking with vicious swipes. Their hilts tangled as, breathing heavily, they glared into one another's face, then in a split second he used his superior strength to wrest the sword from her grasp and send it spinning to the floor. She was helpless, waiting for the blow to the heart that would end her life.

But suddenly Steven was attacked from behind and Mark stood there. 'Fight me, you whoreson coward!'

Steven spun round. There was no time for anything but each man fighting, a desperate dance of slash and feint, sweat beading their faces. Antonia had retrieved her sword and was watching closely. She gasped when Mark slipped, falling to the floor. Steven was upon him, sword raised for the fatal blow.

'Die, you supporter of a tyrant!' he bellowed triumphantly.

'Ashley!' Antonia cried.

He turned momentarily, sword raised, but was too late. Antonia summoned all her strength and her blade entered his chest, the tip appearing between his shoulder-blades. Their eyes met for a second and his were full of astonishment. Then he fell backwards, blood foaming from his lips, and she knew he was dead.

Judith was too busy to think of anything but the wounded who limped in, or those that were aided by comrades. Several women were wailing as their

170

lifeless men were brought to them. She was learning quickly, mopping up blood, attending to bullet wounds or stabs, remembering what she had learned in the still-room, using the skills she had practiced on Antonia. Fortunately the casualties had been few and reports of the outcome were encouraging. Every time she saw an injured person she breathed a sigh of relief because it was not Mark or Antonia, or any of her friends. Her respect for the leaguer women grew and grew.

Then came the good news. Holt Hall had been taken, but it was not yet over. Apparently Prince Rupert had been merciful, as was his way, and the defenders allowed to march out instead of being slaughtered. A Royalist garrison was put in charge, but Judith was filled with anxiety about the fate of Mark. None of those returning from the fray seemed to know. Then after what seemed an eternity he was there, sweeping her into his arms.

Antonia stood beside them, looking at her seriously. 'Your husband is dead.'

'What?' Judith was stunned.

'I killed him in fair fight. I challenged him but was disarmed. To save me Mark joined in but Ashley had him trapped so, having retrieved my weapon, I challenged him and ran him through. He'll bully you no more, Judith.'

'I can't believe it.' She felt guilty because she was so relieved. Surely she shouldn't feel happy because someone was dead?

'It's true,' Mark averred. 'We left the body in the parson's care. He will be transported back to Ferris Mead for burial in the family tomb.'

'What will happen to the house and estate?' Judith clung to Mark's hand. 'There is a Puritan nephew

171

who may take charge, and an honest agent to go on running everything, besides Mrs Moffat and Mr Barnes, but really I suppose it belongs to me.'

'You can't go back there. You will be viewed as a traitor and can only return when the king is restored to his throne.'

'You must return to Oxford with us,' Antonia said firmly.

All around them men were moaning in pain and the army doctors were dealing with them. Cavalry and foot soldiers were returning to camp, and the news was that Rupert would be staying at Holt Hall that night and the army would retire to their various headquarters next day.

Having seen that Judith was safe with Mark, Antonia went to find him.

Order at the manor had been partially restored, the former occupants sent on their way, escorted by their soldiers. Despite what the Roundheads said the Cavaliers treated the women with respect, and there was none of the pillage and rape that Parliamentarian broadsheets liked to print. Antonia left Sultan in the stables and was directed to the prince.

He was dining with his officers. Although the besieged had been running short of food the Royalists had brought provisions with them. There was a general air of a job well done, although Antonia had been aware of a change in Rupert. He was no longer so optimistic and generally short-tempered, driven to distraction by the prevarications of his uncle and his habit of listening to unwise councillors.

'Come in, Antonia,' he said, waving her into a chair. 'It went well today.'

This was the tenor of the conversation, but beneath

his apparent confidence she sensed unease. When the others had gone they sat on, saying little, and later she accompanied him to the master bedroom that was his for the night.

He was unshaven and wearing the clothes he had been in for hours, and looked weary enough to drop. Antonia removed her doublet and lay with him in the oak bed with its tester and posts, and he turned his head and looked at her. 'How goes it with you?'

'Well,' she replied, stroking his stubbly cheek. 'Do you recall Lady Judith, who left her Puritan husband to join our ranks? I killed him today.'

He shifted impatiently. 'Antonia, let us not dwell on what took place here. Can't we forget the war for a few hours?'

Antonia needed no second bidding, unfastening him as he lay on his back, arms laced beneath his head. 'Do it to me,' he growled.

She opened her mouth and descended on his erect cock, running her tongue over its length then taking it in deeply, tasting the salt of his pre-come. He moved his hips impatiently, rushing towards relief. Antonia boiled with need but recognised that he must be brought off first, to relax the tensions of the day. His thrusts became wilder. He had a stranglehold on her hair, keeping her pressed to his groin, and then he suddenly groaned, his spunk filling her mouth and trickling down her chin. She let him gain every ounce of pleasure before gently withdrawing and wiping her face.

He sighed deeply and smiled at her. He wasn't one for words, but she knew he liked her attentions. No longer the unskilled lover he had been when she first shared his bed, he now knew how to pleasure her too, slipping a hand down the front of her breeches and finding her clitoris. It was her turn to lie there and let him bring her to climax, and those royal fingers that had held a sword in defence of the realm were now used on her.

Afterwards they slept, curled up like two spoons, and she knew that if ever there was a man for whom she would forfeit her independence, it would be Prince Rupert.

The leaguer was crowded, women and children greeting their men. In one wagon a young wife was in premature labour brought about by the shock of hearing that her husband was slain. The older women were attending to her, but her moans and screams were a chilling accompaniment to the encroaching darkness.

Emma and Tom were reunited, hanging on to each other in the joy of knowing he had returned. Mark and Judith had nowhere private to go, so they occupied the small space allotted to her at the back of a canvas-covered cart, huddled under his cloak and her shawl and a tattered blanket. It was not the time or place to make love, so they crouched there embracing, and finally slept.

The wail of a newborn baby brought relief to those listening out for the labouring mother. All was well. The camp quietened, lit by the smouldering logs fuelling the fire in the centre of the wagon circle.

Judith woke, aware that a bird was heralding the dawn. Mark was sleepily kissing her face, and as she came more fully awake she could feel his hand under her skirt, his fingers combing through her pubic bush. She turned into him, denying all thought of Steven's death, only knowing that Mark was her love and she wanted to consummate that feeling. The floor of the

174

cart was hard, the air cold and their covering inadequate, but their need for one another surpassed all that.

Just for that small space of time they explored and caressed, kissed and tongued, shameless in their desire. He bared her breasts, the nipples rendered hard as cherry stones with the chill and the feel of his fingers. She in turn held his rock-hard penis in her hand, fondling it from base to dome, smearing it with the dew that seeped from its single eye. He mounted her once he had brought her to bliss, entering her slippery channel and thrusting like a man possessed.

The sun was rising as, replete, they cuddled together for a few precious moments before the camp began to stir.

Mark had to leave her, returning to his regiment and preparing for the march towards Oxford or wherever his commander dictated. 'If Rupert ordered us to go to Timbuktu we would obey,' he said, trying to lighten the sorrow of parting again.

'I wish this was all over,' she whispered. 'Will life ever be normal again?'

'Have faith in the future, dear heart. You have already come through many trials and we are still here, in each other's arms. It was meant to be.' He freed himself from her, picking up his sword. 'Now I must go to my men, and you to help the women. We should be moving back to Oxford today.'

Several weeks later Isobel was immersed in the bathtub set up in her dressing-room. The servants had filled it with hot water and she was relaxing, head resting on the rim, eyes closed. There was much to occupy her thoughts although, with her carefree nature, she was inclined not to worry. Instead she lifted her lids and stared at Jamie, who striped naked, was about to join her.

'Wouldn't it be wonderful if one day houses could be fitted with permanent baths, attached to flowing water taps, both hot and cold, and with a drainage system by which it could be emptied?' she remarked, adding, as he stepped between her parted thighs, 'and big enough for two.'

He smiled at her, on his knees now. 'But this is so intimate. Give me the sponge, dearest, so I may wash. I smell like a fisherman's doxy. We've been kept busy, my unit guarding Oxford while the main part of the army is in the north, fighting at a place called Naseby. Antonia is there with her troops. We're awaiting news.'

She sat up to give him more room, her legs on either side of him. He was so handsome a man, with his brown hair tied back and his body hardened by constant activity. He had not long returned from the latest skirmish in the area, but was worried, as was every Royalist, by the continuing success of the Roundheads. The king had ridden out to join Rupert and siege the town of Leicester, and all were hoping for a favourable outcome.

Jamie finished washing and threw the sponge at Isobel playfully, then leaned over to kiss her breasts. She responded eagerly, slipping her hand between his legs, caressing his balls and prick. In an instant it hardened and rose, a sight that never failed to excite her.

The steaming perfumed water added to her sense of wellbeing. Jamie was one of many lovers, but she had a special place in her heart for him, always relieved when he returned home safely. And he usually brought good news of Antonia and her friends, who by some miracle always came back.

As he knelt before her she took his face in her hands and kissed him fondly.

'I've never made love in the bath before,' she confessed, and rose slightly, encouraging him to sit while she positioned herself over him, the water and her own juices combining to ease his entrance into her body. This was one of Isobel's happiest moments, surrounded by luxury and with an equally ardent partner. She could banish all thoughts of the dangers that now threatened Royalist supporters, confident that whatever happened her mode of life would continue.

Jamie ran his hands over her back and shoulders, bending forward to take her nipples into his mouth, one by one. She reached beneath the water to her open sex, and whilst gently rising and falling on his engorged member used her fingers on her clitoris. The water slopped around them, spilling over onto the carpet as their passion took over. But on the brink of coming she suddenly pulled away. 'Let us go to bed,' she whispered huskily. 'I can't give full rein to my feelings here.'

They grabbed towels and wrapped in them ran to the bedroom. There, beneath the warm coverlet, she arched her pelvis and opened herself to his gaze as she finished masturbating, climaxing with a cry and urging him to enter her.

He was beyond control, plunging and bucking in the manner she so enjoyed. Women had their own particular charm, but there was nothing quite like a rampant male, and Jamie was certainly that. She doubted that she would be able to sit comfortable after he'd finished with her, but even this idea was pleasurable. Within seconds she felt the warm outpouring of his tribute and he slumped on her, his heart pounding.

'Oh, that was good!' she cried, holding him close and enjoying the aftermath. 'I wish we could live forever, never changing or growing old, staying just as we are now.'

'You know that to be a dream,' he said. 'We must enjoy while we are able.'

Judith was with the leaguer after the Royalists had been routed at Naseby. She huddled with the women and children, hearing the sound of triumphant laugher and cheering as the Roundhead soldiers broke into the camp. Some of the screaming women were seized and she watched, horrified, as they were called whores while their faces were being slashed. Bleeding, sobbing, they were manhandled and abused.

A pair of men, their eyes alight with fanatical hatred, grabbed Judith, their daggers raised to destroy her beauty forever. She kicked and struggled in vain while one of them shouted, 'Royalist harlot! Service the troops, do you? We'll make sure no man ever looks at you again!'

Then as the knife touched her nose, ready to slice it off, she heard hooves and a furious voice and was swept up onto Mark's horse as, ignoring attempts to stop him, he galloped off with her. She never knew how they succeeded in breaking through the enemy and reaching open country, but by some miracle they did it. Eventually they paused in a wooded valley and he lowered her to the grass.

'Emma's still there.' This was all she could think about. 'And she's with child.'

'There is nothing we can do. Tom is resourceful

and Antonia still alive, but it was a crushing defeat. That man Cromwell has a force to be reckoned with in his New Model Army, and Sir Thomas Fairfax led them and he's a fine soldier.'

'Where's Prince Rupert?' She couldn't stop trembling.

'He's retreated with most of his men, and getting the king to safety. Fighting on was pointless. Now you and I must journey to Oxford.'

'It's so far,' she wailed, worn out by travelling and setting up camp and seeing the Royalists defeated.

Though they had successfully taken the city of Leicester the behaviour of her own side had appalled her, with the slaughter if so many innocent citizens and all the worst aspects of war. Usually Rupert was merciful, but not there, and she had begun to doubt his leadership.

'I know, but we will get there,' Mark soothed. 'Stopping at farmhouses, perhaps, resting and eating. I have money and this always talks.'

The weather was warm and there was no rain, and after letting the horse graze for a while they continued their journey. Mark had travelled around enough by now to know the way, and how to trade with innkeepers on route. He hid the fact that they were part of the army so soundly beaten at Naseby, for news of this was trickling through. To all intents and purposes they were a married couple on their way to a funeral.

Too shocked by the dire results of the battle they talked little, consoled one another by nights spent in tavern beds, but were intent on getting to the university town.

Chapter 11

'Madame, let me help you leave this wretched, war-torn country. I have my own vessel waiting for me in Dover, and would be delighted to escort you to Paris,' proclaimed the elegant French beau in his near perfect English, with just the hint of an accent.

With this idea in mind Isobel had been encouraging him recently, giving him more and more access to her house and, lately, to her bed. It was high time she departed. The Parliamentarians were winning, without a doubt. Prince Rupert had just surrendered Bristol and the king, furious, had sent him into exile. Oxford would be the next city to be attacked, for they wanted to capture Charles.

She gave Comte Henri Dubois her most seductive smile. 'I shall be pleased to accept your generous offer, *monsieur*. I have property and money there, and have been thinking of leaving for some time. May I bring a friend with me?'

'Certainly, *ma belle*.' Henri kissed her fingers, and then moved to the inside of her wrist, his narrow moustache providing a delicious tickling sensation. 'There will be room for your servants, carriages and baggage. Is your friend female?'

'Indeed, and very beautiful.' Isobel was thinking of Judith. She'd already had this out with Antonia, who refused to abandon Rupert. 'I'm sure you will find her most agreeable. She's brave, too, and was a she-soldier fighting for the king, but has lately been with the wagons and had a bad experience at the battle of Naseby.'

He slid an arm around her and they relaxed on the

couch. 'Let us lay our plans for departure,' he said, lifting her skirt and exposing her small feet in spindle-heeled shoes and her legs in fine silk stockings. These were fastened just above the knee by garters with diamanté buckles.

'Not quite yet,' she murmured. 'Haven't we unfinished business here?'

He needed no second bidding, and soon she was leaning over the back of the couch while he entered her from behind. He was a skilled lover and, like her, enjoyed the snugness of anal penetration, but was a dab hand at clitoral stimulation too. Eyes closed, Isobel dwelt on the wonderful sensations he was giving her, but a corner of her mind was occupied with the problem of persuading Judith to leave England with her.

After she and Henri had finished she gathered herself together and sent a messenger to Antonia's headquarters, and within the hour Judith had joined them. Isobel welcomed her with open arms. 'Dearest, how are you? I'm so pleased you are here, in comparative safety. Meet my friend, Comte Henri Dubois. Henri, this is Lady Judith Ashley.'

He bowed low, lifting Judith's hand and planting a kiss on the back of it. 'Charmed, Madame.'

Judith could not restrain her tears, the worries of the last days swamping her. Isobel was so kind, and she poured out her troubles. 'Everything is going wrong. Prince Rupert is off to Europe and Mark is going with him. There is some scheme afoot of the prince becoming a pirate and attacking Roundhead shipping. And Mark wants to join him, Antonia. There is no place for me in their plans. What am I to do? I have no money and can't return to Ferris Mead.'

'Henri has kindly offered that I travel to France aboard his boat. Come with us. Don't worry about money; I have plenty in Paris and a house to live in. You are more likely to see Mark there than if you stay in England.'

'He wants us to be married, but I can't do that yet. I haven't been widowed long enough.'

'There you are then. The problem is solved. You will live with me until such time as he returns from his adventuring with the prince, and we can arrange a grand wedding.' Once launched on an idea Isobel was unstoppable, and Judith had no alternative but to agree. Later she sought Mark, and weeping in his arms, told him what Isobel has suggested.

'I'm glad,' he replied, hugging her to him. 'Now I can go with a quiet mind, knowing you will be safe. Prince Maurice, Rupert's brother, will be coming with us, and we should be able to assist the cause by taking money and goods from the Parliamentary shipping. It will help Prince Charles to survive in Paris where he is living on the goodwill of the young King Louis. His mother is there too, our queen, Henrietta Maria, and all are in need of financial aid. It is my duty to sail with Rupert.'

Oh, men! Judith sighed within herself, their sense of duty meant far more to them than the love of women, yet it was a fault she admired in Mark. He was an honourable person, unlike her dead husband.

'When are you going?' she asked, wishing she could keep him a prisoner forever.

'Within the week.' He sounded as sad as she did, then tried to cheer her by adding, 'When we meet up in Paris after I've been at sea for a while, we shall be able to marry and have that splendid wedding Isobel has promised.'

'Is this our last night together?' she mourned.

'You could look at it in that way, or maybe think of it as the first of many more to come,' he answered wisely, and led her to the bed where she cried and laughed and made frantic love to him.

The vessel was at anchor in the harbour, and Henri's party embarked early on a fine morning in the middle of September. It was a trading ship used for one of his businesses, and was fortunately large, for there were carriages, passengers and baggage to be stowed abroad. Isobel was in her element, but Judith found it hard, missing Mark who had already joined Prince Rupert somewhere in Europe. The voyage was choppy and seasickness added to her misery, and then, pale and wan, she was finally transported to Paris. To her the whole journey had been a nightmare and it was a relief to occupy a guestroom in Isobel's grand mansion in the best part of the French capital.

Isobel had made contact with Tom and Emma and their new baby, and taken them along as members of her staff, making him head groom, but Frankie and Jamie had thrown in their lot with Rupert.

Judith was supplied with a helpful maid who could speak English, and left to recover. When she finally came to herself it was to be aware of the strangeness of her situation, the foreign voice all around her, the different food, and the bells of Paris ringing out. There was a lightness in the air, different to England, which had been at war for so long. The people seemed happy and optimistic. It began to brush off on her.

Isobel had given her clothing; petticoats, chemises, night attire, cloaks, hats and gowns, but now she had decided to take her to the dressmakers to be fitted

183

properly. 'Don't worry about the money,' she said, when Judith expostulated at the cost. 'I have a plan and you will assist me. I intent to turn my mansion into a House of Sale.'

'What is that? I don't understand.'

'Oh, you innocent! A bordello, darling, a high-class brothel,' Isobel laughed. 'I shall entertain all the best people in Paris, men and women, and we'll make a mint of money.'

'Really? Is this proper? I thought that whores were despised.'

'Don't be silly. You lived among them in the leaguer. Didn't they provide capital service for the frustrated soldiers?' Isobel was highly amused, pirouetting before the mirror in Judith's room. 'You could say that I am a whore, but of the upper variety, known as a courtesan, and I do it because I enjoy it, not through necessity. Come, don your cloak. We are off to the shops.'

The streets of Paris were as dirty as those of any city, strewn with garbage, horse manure and human excrement, but the areas occupied by the aristocrats were cobbled and paved. The squares where churches stood, and bookshops, picture galleries and exclusive tailors and milliners plied their trades, were clean and well cared for. Isobel's carriage pulled up outside a couturiers. Judith had never visited such a place before. It was elegance personified, and had bay windows with diamond panes and tubs of flowers.

They were welcomed by the owner, Madame Blanchard. Curtsying she greeted Isobel. 'Baroness, how delightful! It is so long since you visited my humble establishment.'

'I have been in England, but the war is becoming tiresome and I missed Paris,' Isobel said casually, and this shocked Judith when she recalled the conflict, the suffering and her own part in it. 'Now let me see the latest innovations, and my friend, Lady Ashley, is interested too.'

The shop was spacious, carpeted, and furnished with small gilt chairs for clients to occupy. There were shelves with bales of material, all exquisite and costly, and mannequins, three foot high dolls, dressed á la mode. Madame clapped her hands and two smart assistants appeared from the rear, and in a short while Judith found herself borne into a curtained cubicle with one of them following, her arms piled with various garments. Isobel occupied the one next to it, and her excited squeals indicated her delight in the gowns she was trying on.

Judith lost any shyness as she was undressed and laced into one lovely gown after another. The new style consisted of a tight bodice worn over a busk that pushed her breasts high, baring them almost to the nipples, with puffy elbow-length sleeves slipping from the shoulders as if pulled by their own weight. The skirts were full, worn over several lace-trimmed petticoats.

'Whatever you fancy, dearest,' called Isobel over the screen that separated them. 'We must make an impression at the first party I shall be holding in the near future.'

'I'm sure there will be no doubt of that,' said a male voice, and Henri walked in to where Judith was standing in nothing but her chemise, between changing from one gown into the next.

She clutched the flimsy undergarment to her, surprised by his sudden appearance. He was superbly attired in a black velvet doublet laced with silver, straight breeches decorated with buttons down the outer seams, and knee-high boots with scarlet heels and welts. He wore a sword at his left hip and carried a slender walking cane. His hat had a wide brim and ostrich feathers. His cloak was short and swirling, lined with scarlet and sporting a large collar.

He smiled at Judith, doffed his hat and bowed. 'You resemble a shy wood nymph, startled whilst at her toilette,' he said, making no apology and settling himself on a chair. He crossed one knee over the other and continued to study her.

Madame popped her head through the curtain and said, 'Good morning, Comte Dubois.'

He kissed his fingertips to her and then Isobel joined in. 'Henri, what are you doing, spying on us? You know you should only see us when we are wearing our new dresses, not while trying to decide which one to purchase.'

'I came to offer my advice. You know I have a sense of style second to none.'

'Sense of fiddlesticks!' she answered tartly, and disappeared again.

Judith was not sure how to behave. There was little doubt that she owed Henri for his willingness to transport her in his vessel. While on board, and since, he had shown interest in her and she found him attractive, but was feeling too ill to think about it. Now were it not for her commitment to Mark she might have taken him as a lover. He was watching her as the shop assistant helped her into yet another gown. This was of rose-pink satin and flattering. She wanted it.

Henri was obviously enjoying the spectacle. 'Allow me to add its cost to my account,' he said, reaching out and taking her hand.

His touch was like sudden fire in her belly, making

her aware of how much she was missing male attention, her bed so lonely and life lacking that certain glow a lover brings. She was suddenly angry with Mark for leaving her, no longer lovelorn but indignant. There had been no word from him and she wondered why she was bothering to remain faithful. Henri was everything a woman could desire, handsome, titled, rich and intelligent. Why deny him for the sake of someone who might never appear in her life again? Isobel's carefree attitude towards love and amatory encounters was beginning to rub off on Judith.

She returned Henri's smile, murmuring, 'I couldn't possibly let you pay for my gown. Isobel has kindly offered to lend me the money.'

'Nonsense,' he averred, standing and slipping the assistant a coin to leave them. 'Accept it as an early birthday present, if you like, or as a welcome gift for coming to my country.'

He put his arms around her and held her against him, her face pressed into the velvet doublet. She was aware of a sudden rush of desire. He felt warm and comforting and smelled deliciously of orange flower water. But not here, she decided, not in a cubicle like this, where Madame probably received generous tips for letting amorous gentlemen play Peeping Tom.

She felt his smooth-shaven cheek against hers, and the sensation of his moustache as he kissed her, a soft, exploring kiss to which she responded by parting her lips. One of his hands cupped her breast, and she could feel him hardening.

Freeing herself, she said, 'I should be no more than a common slut if I yielded to you so quickly.'

He understood, giving her a charming smile. 'You would have me woo you? Take you to the theatre,

187

perhaps, or to the races, or invite you to my house to dine?'

'That would be nice. It has never happened to me, you see. Until I ran away from my Puritan husband I hadn't experienced such things.'

'Indeed? I would enjoy listening to you recounting your adventures.' He was so nice that Judith's scruples were melting like snow in sunlight.

He recalled the assistant and Judith undressed before him and donned her outer clothing. Isobel, too, had made a selection and Madame promised to have the articles delivered next day.

True to his word, Henri took Judith to the theatre late that afternoon. He had a stage box and she was enthralled, having never seen a performance in her life. She was surprised to see women on the candlelit boards, flaunting their beauty and talent.

'In England men take female roles. It is considered unseemly for ladies to show themselves off. Only during masques at Court do genteel women join in.'

Henri pulled a face. 'I know, and the theatres are closed owing to the war. I missed such entertainment.'

Judith could not understand what was being said, for her grasp of the language was sketchy, but Henri explained the plot and she stared at the well-dressed crowd who occupied the pit, upper circle or boxes like his. There were two intervals during which he ordered wine, nodding to several acquaintances, and made her feel at ease. Sitting back to enjoy the show she was aware that his hand rested on her knee, softly exploring, gently sliding her skirt up. Her heart was starting to pound as he found the silky skin of her thigh above her stocking top. The actors were declaiming, but she could not concentrate, her clitoris responding as he began to stroke it.

She knew she should push him away, but her need for fulfilment was too great. The whole escapade was new and exciting, offering a glimpse of what life could be like there, totally different to that which she had known at Ferris Mead or when fighting for the king. This was comprised of ease and luxury and the fine things of life. Henri was offering her a glimpse of how it could be for her. Besides which, she was but human and had been denied male attention for weeks now. Oh she could pleasure herself and, had she told her, no doubt Isobel would have taken her to bed, but having tasted the fruits of the Tree of Knowledge this would not prove enough. She needed an ardent man.

Seated alone with Henri in the intimacy of the box she parted her legs, allowing him to explore her inner secrets. He took her hand and guided it to the swelling in his breeches, letting her know that he, too, was desirous. Sitting there as prim as a nun, her face remained impassive as he brought her to climax. They were shielded from the crystal chandeliers that hung over the auditorium, and the attention of the audience was riveted on the stage.

Henri unlaced his breeches and moved her hand to take the heat and hardness of his cock, and she did not hesitate to grant him the pleasure he had just given her. It was over quickly, his tribute caught in the handkerchief he drew from his pocket. Judith managed to convince herself that this act in no way proved disloyalty to Mark, as Henri had not entered her body. Nonetheless she found it hard to meet his eyes when, the show over, they left the theatre to enter his coach, waiting outside for them.

He took her to Isobel's house, climbing out and

seeing her to the door, then giving her a chaste kiss on the cheek and leaving with the promise of driving her to the park next day. She was surprised, yet pleased he was not taking an advantage.

'That's what he is like,' said Isobel, after Judith had talked of her adventure. Then she changed the subject. 'And now, my dear, let me tell you what I have done so far to open my Temple of Venus. The decorators will be in to smarten it up, and I've engaged the services of Lola Diago to advise me.'

'Who is she?' Judith found it hard to keep up with her.

'One of the most popular courtesans in town. Although France is a Roman Catholic country, she tells me that she has several priests among her clients. We shall encourage them, and men of letters, artists, politicians and musicians, making sure they can gamble at cards, if they so desire, listen to music, dance and be entertained by lovely ladies or beautiful boys, according to their preference.'

'And what part do I play?' Judith was still confused.

'You, my dove, will be a hostess, although if you wish you may pleasure someone. There are skills you need to learn and Henri will be only too eager to show you. Don't look so worried. I'm sure you will find the lessons enjoyable.'

As promised Henri called for Judith next day. He was driving an open-topped curricle, a light, fast vehicle drawn by two spirited horses. 'The park is a fashionable place in which to see and be seen,' he informed her as they passed similar equipage on the way there. 'Sometimes we pit our nags against one another, betting on the outcome. There is money to be won.'

It was a crisp, cloudless morning and she was intrigued by the elegantly dressed people strolling there, and children with their nursemaids, as well as dandies exchanging gossip and flirting. Is this what it had been like in the London parks before the war? She wondered, never having visited there. Refreshments were served from booths, wine and ale and that recent import, coffee.

'Try a cup,' Henri urged. 'It is most beneficial, especially after a hard night on the town.'

She did so, finding it bitter to her taste buds, but pretending otherwise to appear worldly in his eyes. He smiled and she remembered Isobel's suggestion that he would have other things to teach her. They returned to that lady's house, for she had invited him to take lunch with them. This was an informal, gay affair, with both Henri and Isobel exchanging witticisms and speculating on the latest scandals.

After the meal Isobel stretched and yawned. 'Siesta time. I enjoy a nap in the afternoon. It refreshes me for the evening entertainments.' She handed Henri a riding whip and added, 'Why don't you take him to your chamber, Judith?'

Ah, Judith thought, so this is what it has been leading to. I am to have my first instructions, and he will be my teacher. She nodded in agreement, certain that he would not pressure her into doing anything she found distasteful.

'Well, sir, and what will my lesson be today? I assume that is why we're here,' she said haughtily, as her bedroom door closed behind them.

Henri looked at her. 'Are you sure you want to do this?'

'It rather depends on what it is, but I'm certain that

Isobel would not have suggested anything harmful.'

'You are right.' He removed his doublet, loosened his collar and opened his shirt. The whiteness of the linen emphasised his swarthy complexion. It added to his attraction, and she could imagine him duelling or charging into battle on a thoroughbred stallion.

He stood looking at her, hands on his hips. Judith was embarrassed, not knowing where to start. 'What would you have me do?' she asked nervously.

'Undress, but leave on your stockings and shoes. Then order me to lie on the bed. Use this on me if I appear tardy,' he handed her the whip. 'I shall call you *mistress*. I have been bad and need correction.'

She could not fail to notice the swelling in his crotch, as if the very words aroused him. Having been afraid that she was the one to be punished, she now mused on what it would be like to wield the instrument herself, inflicting pain. Or could it be pleasure Henri would experience? She had witnessed that at the first of Isobel's orgies without understanding it.

Henri stripped off his clothes and she admired his body, wide at the shoulders and tapering down to a supple waist, narrow hips and long, muscular legs. He already had an erection, and this in itself was impressive.

He handed her a bundle of cords and stretched on the bed, lying on his back, arms wide and reaching towards the head-posts, and his legs pointing in the direction of those at the foot. Judith took off everything except her stockings and shoes, as instructed. A glimpse in the mirror showed her a wanton woman, her hair falling about her face and the whip in her hand. She flicked it, and the effect was exciting.

I can do this, she thought. I might even enjoy it.

She strode towards Henri and, under his direction, knotted the cords around his wrists and tied them to the posts, then did the same to his ankles. He was securely tethered and helpless, and she remembered the feeling when Steven had treated her thus. She had been frightened and uncomfortable, but Henri's erection grew even larger.

'Oh, mistress, you are so beautiful and the ropes feel wonderful. I have been a naughty boy, and need to be chastised,' he begged.

Judith hesitated, and then lifted the whip and flicked him across the thighs. She failed to comprehend why anyone should find this arousing. 'Why have you been bad?' she asked, taking another stroke, to his chest this time. A red stripe was forming from her first attempt.

'Oh, you know, mistress. I've cheated at cards and been with low women. Strike me again for mercy's sake! Tell me I am a villain!'

She caught the glint of laughter in his eyes and could not be sure if he was sincere, yet the state of his manhood suggested otherwise. So taking a deep breath she scolded, 'You're a scoundrel, sir! A disgrace to your family name!'

'That's good!' he encouraged. 'More insults if you please, mistress. And implement them with the whip.'

She was getting accustomed to the sound of leather meeting bare flesh, and if he found it stimulating then all well and good. She raked around in her mind for insults exchanged among the soldiers, and came out with, 'You're a bastard, a filthy dog! A snotty-nosed, pox-ridden piece of shit!'

Getting into the spirit of it she whipped him again

and again, substituting Steven's face for his, and those of the Roundheads who had wanted to mar her beauty forever and use her for their lust. She was sweating and aroused, beginning to enjoy the experience.

Henri was moaning in earnest. 'I'm sorry, mistress! Oh God, I need you to bring me off! Please, please, rub my cock!'

She gritted her teeth and lashed down the whip with all her strength. He cried out, and then she was merciful, bending over him and taking his engorged penis in her hand. 'Is this what you want?' she crooned, stopping for a second. 'Shall mistress let you come? You naughty boy.'

'Oh yes, yes!' It seemed Henri was in earnest, displaying a side of his nature she had never suspected, and a need in some men she did not know existed until that afternoon. It was a revelation, making her feel powerful.

He was straining towards her, his cock huge, the helm a fiery red. Judith could no longer resist it, using her hands in ways she had not realised she knew. She caressed his balls, jiggled them a little, and then concentrated on giving him the most rewarding orgasm. Strangely she did not need one herself, content on bringing him joy, and he slumped back after filling her hand with his libation.

Then he smiled up at her. 'That was well done. You are an apt pupil, *ma belle*. Now, please untie me.'

An imp of mischief suggested that she refuse, leaving him there, but she didn't have quite enough courage, as yet. Later, perhaps, if she did this to clients she might add to their stress, or joy as the case might be, but she liked Henri and did as he requested. He sat up, rubbing his wrists and ankles.

'Would you like me to spend more time with you? Perhaps give you the enjoyment you have just lavished on me?'

'That isn't necessary,' she answered. 'I can now understand how women can do this purely for money. Love is what inspires me, and at the moment I am waiting to hear from Mark.'

'He is a lucky man,' Henri said, kissing her cheek and rising. 'Will you at least allow me to take you to the theatre again? There's a comedy this afternoon. If we hurry we can be there by four.'

'Won't you be sore?' She pointed to the red stripes scoring his body.

He grinned, viewing them in the mirror. 'Yes I shall feel them, and be reminded of you. I think you are going to be an asset to Isobel's Temple of Venus.'

Chapter 12

Judith was beginning to find it almost impossible to reconcile her present mode of life to that which she had experienced in the Royalist army. Had she really fought and slept rough, been in mortal danger and come out of it unharmed? Sometimes she dreamed of battles and hardship and the comrades who had protected her, but it was all fading into a blur. Even the memory of Mark's face was becoming indistinct, though concern for him and his whereabouts continued to torment her.

The Temple of Venus was ready for the opening. Isobel had spent a lot of money on having it refurbished, and news of its existence spread among the nobility. There was an atmosphere of excitement and anticipation when the doors were opened at last. Maids in short skirts and low bodices had been enlisted to serve the guests, and handsome footmen wearing nothing but loincloths walked around with trays holding glasses of wine. The gaming room had been prepared for the use of the gamblers, and a string orchestra installed on a stage at one end of the ballroom.

The mansion was set in its own grounds, and the drive was lit by flares. Carriages started to arrive, and Isobel and Judith were at the imposing entrance to welcome the guests. Isobel was attired as the goddess, Venus Aphrodite, wearing a semi-transparent white gown in the style of Ancient Greece, with sandals on her bare feet and her hair piled high. Judith's was similar, and she felt naked under the perusal of so many eyes.

Most of those invited wore fancy-dress, and some sported masks. There were ladies in harem costume, others in nuns' habits, and some pretending to be bacchantes in brief tunics and goat skins. The men had come as Turks, monks and centurions, and a few were wearing female apparel. Refreshments were served in the reception room and wine flowed freely.

Judith conversed with them, having been taught how to do so by Isobel and Henri. While they were still sober the talk was of clothes, their estates in the country, and she even caught some of the men discussing politics and business. Above the chatter she heard the pure, unearthly strains of the castrati who had been hired to sing. It was all similar to her first visit to Isobel's house in Oxford, but now she was no longer a green girl, and the things she witnessed did not shock her.

196

'Wine, madame?' one of the footmen asked, and by now she could talk their language, though not fluently, then he added meaningfully, 'Or can I offer you something more?'

He was classically handsome, handpicked by Lola for the job. A collar studded with spikes fitting his neck closely. From this stretched thongs that crossed his chest, where gold rings glinted in his pierced nipples. The cloth that covered his loins was cut in such a way that his large cock was partly exposed, and his buttocks were bare, divided by the narrowest of gussets.

Judith placed a hand on his forearm. The skin was golden-brown and furry. It felt good and she was tempted, and then remembered that this was part of his job, and that he would earn extra money from amorous women. He was a male prostitute, and she lost interest, simply taking a glass from his tray.

'It's a great success,' Isobel enthused in passing. She was on the arm of a Roman emperor in a toga.

'Indeed, it seems to be,' Judith responded.

She was more interested in observing rather than joining in. She had been instructed to make sure that everyone was getting what they wanted, and it seemed that they were, especially as the evening wore on, the wine went down and inhibitions disappeared.

Several of the women wore black riding boots with high heels over stockings upheld by sparkling garters. Their skirts were miniscule, showing their naked rumps, and were also made of leather, as were their corsets. They strode about arrogantly, swishing their long whips. Some of the men seemed fascinated by them, and Judith was vividly reminded of the lesson she'd had with Henri. Within a short time these dominating females had retired with their partners, only to return after a while in search of more victims.

A large man wearing a cassock opened over a huge belly and erect cock was seated in an alcove. Several ladies, nearly nude, were waiting their turn to go over his knee and be spanked. Those who had already enjoyed this were displaying their bottoms, rendered pink by the force of his hand. They were fully aroused, rubbing themselves to climax.

'Come to my tent in the desert, and we will make passionate love under an Eastern moon,' said a dramatic voice close to her ear. It was Henri in the garb of an Arabian sheik, the burnoose and head-cloth suiting his dark skin. 'Are you enjoying the spectacle?'

'Yes, although I'm surprised that people of rank and position should amuse themselves in such a manner.'

'People are but human all the world over, be they peasants or princes. The latter are more inclined to indulge their lusts, having money and opportunity. Don't be deceived by rank, *cherie*. Come, let us dance.'

The musicians in the ballroom had started out playing gavottes and the stately pavane, but the dancers were becoming rowdy, demanding jigs, skipping and jumping, the men whirling their partners off their feet. Couples were fornicating in full view of everyone, though some had disappeared to more private places. Isobel had put bedchambers at their disposal.

'Have you been to the punishment room tonight?' Henri asked, above the clamour.

'Not yet.' Judith was curious to see what was taking place there, having helped to prepare it.

198

In a lower part of the house it was dimly lit and warmed by a brazier. It was busy. She saw a girl in a wedding gown and veil bound to a post, while her so-called bridegroom pulled her bodice down to her waist and bit her nipples. She struggled against her bonds, but was moaning with pleasure. A woman was slung in chains, naked and helpless, while one man had his cock in her mouth and another was taking his pleasure between her legs. Two others stood on each side of her, and her hands were occupied with rubbing their penises.

'*Mon dieu*! They are keeping her busy,' Henri chuckled.

Judith watched, fascinated, as one of the leather-clad women stood over a man who cringed at her feet while she plied her whip to his bare back. A tall catamite in a dress bared his rump to a stout friar who spat on his hand, applied it to the young man's rectum and then inserted his cock. Wherever Judith looked it was to see people indulging in their fantasies. In fact no one appeared to be having straightforward sex.

'What do you think of this?' Henri murmured in her ear, his breath raising the fine down on her body and waking her desires.

'I'm confused,' she answered, unable to resist pressing back against him as he leaned against the wall, supporting her. 'But then, at the first party I attended given by Isobel I saw similar things. That's where I met Mark.'

He gave her an impatient little shake. 'Oh, Mark! Put him out of your mind. It's months since you have seen him, isn't it? I'll wager that he hasn't remained faithful to you.'

He was voicing her worst fears and it filled her

with pain and also defiance. His arms were about her, holding her tightly, and she could feel him hardening under the burnoose. She did not stop him when his hand descended lower, rubbing her clit through her thin robe. It was a delicious frottage and she pressed on his finger. Meanwhile his lips were caressing her neck and shoulders and that sensitive spot at the top of her spine. She was seduced by this, and also by the noises and actions of those enjoying their unusual forms of pleasure. Nothing seemed to matter but the fulfilment of the senses.

Mark. He had abandoned her. The news was that Rupert had set up a fleet and was harassing Roundhead shipping, taking Mark, Antonia and Jamie with him. Why should I curtail my activities? Judith thought angrily. Mark could surely have sent a message to me somehow?

The light was dim there and she could almost pretend that nothing was happening as Henri lifted her robe. She could feel him nudging his organ between her buttocks, seeking entrance. Meanwhile his finger persisted in its arousal, but now there was no fabric in the way. He was stroking her wet labia and nubbin, and with a sigh of resignation she let him penetrate her, and the slow in and out movement augmented the sensations she was already feeling. He was so good, so experienced a lover, unhurried, making sure his partner was on the road to orgasm, and Judith forgot Mark for a moment.

'You are beautiful,' Henri gasped as she reached her climax and he gave vent to his.

Judith relaxed in his arms, her robe covering her again. 'This is between you and me,' she warned.

'Of course, *ma petite*,' he promised, then led her back to the party and looked after her for the rest of

200

the evening.

This is the best time of my life, Antonia thought,
seated in the main cabin of Rupert's vessel, which
was harassing Parliamentary shipping off the coast of
Ireland. He was in charge and she was his secretary,
as well as taking part in the action. Mark was captain
of a further ship of the small fleet, and Jamie served
under Prince Maurice who commanded another.

When they first left England Rupert had rounded
up exiled Royalists, formed a troop and joined the
French army. Then came the chance of fighting for
the king, who was now on the run, by robbing the
Roundheads and supply money for the penniless
royal family living at St Germaine and supported by
kind-hearted relatives.

Antonia was in her element, feeling she was doing
something positive, but more than that she was in
close contact with Rupert. Now he was seated
opposite her, long legs stretched out, booted feet
crossed at the ankles and resting on the table while
the ship rose and fell gently beneath them. He was
dictating a letter to his cousin, Prince Charles. It
wasn't something he enjoyed.

She studied his face while he brooded on what to
say next. He looked older, growing up fast after so
much responsibility, but was still remarkably
handsome, his skin rendered darker by exposure to
the sea air and the sun. He was not a good sailor, and
suffered from mal de mar, and this did not improve
his already irascible temper. But she had learned how
to deal with him, often deliberately exchanging hot
words if he needed to have an argument with
someone.

Antonia missed Isobel and Judith, but had little

time for repining, her life taken up with Rupert. She did not occupy the position of his mistress. As far as the others were aware she was simply one of his aides. Completely caught up in his desire to help his uncle he had little time for dalliance and bed for him meant sleep. He used the state room and she had a space no bigger than a cupboard in which to lay her head. Even so, she would rather be there than anywhere.

Life was turbulent. When news came of an English ship heading their way they would lie in wait and attack it, firing a shot across its bows. Rupert always led the boarding party, quickly capturing the vessel and stripping it of money and goods. These could be sold to aid the cause. Several of the British fleet had come over to their side as they had not been paid by the Parliamentarians. Antonia enjoyed swinging by a rope from her ship to the enemy one, landing on the deck and engaging in fighting, should the enemy captain prove uncooperative. When they saw Rupert they usually surrendered.

But this was not good enough for him. He stopped dictating, dropping his head into his hands and saying, 'I want to rescue my uncle.'

'Is this possible?' She hated to see him distressed. 'Do you now where he is hiding?'

He got up and strode about the cabin, remembering to duck his tall head to avoid the beams. 'There are rumours he is in Ireland or the Isle of Wight, but nothing is certain. I shall have to return to Paris soon, taking money to Prince Charles. He is growing into a fine lad and eager to raise an army and attack England, but this is not possible yet. Our resources are low.'

Paris! Antonia immediately thought of Isobel, in no

doubt that she was making a success of whatever venture she had decided to undertake. A stab of longing pierced her. She missed her company, her frivolity and waywardness, her seductive body. How good it would be to indulge in a proper bath instead of a quick dip in the cold sea, and then to take her ease in Isobel's chamber.

Rupert was susceptible to the feelings of others, looking at her sharply. 'You want to return there?'

'Yes, Highness,' she replied truthfully. 'We have been at sea for months. Don't you feel the need of a break from fighting?'

'I'm a soldier, or a pirate,' he added with a grin. 'I've been a soldier most of my life. I was troublesome at home, so they tell me, called Rupert the Devil then, and mother sent me off to join the army at thirteen. What else do I know?' His face darkened. 'She always preferred her dogs and horses to her children, and there were over a dozen of us. Her faithful admirers call her The Queen of Hearts, and are forever trying to get back her kingdom for her.'

'You're a splendid soldier.' She wanted to encourage him. 'But don't you want to settle down one day, marry a princess and raise a family?'

He shrugged. 'I should be bored to distraction. No, a soldier I am, and a soldier I always will be.'

Greatly daring, she stood close to him, looking up into his face, unable to hide the admiration in her eyes. 'Once you asked me to help you forget the conflict for a while. Can't we do that now?'

'I trust you are not getting sentimental about me,' he warned, but did not withdraw when she put her arms around him. 'I can't offer you anything except hardship and possible death.'

'That is my choice, Highness,' and holding his hand she led him towards the state room.

Once inside he became a changed man, seizing her roughly and propelling her towards the narrow bed. He seemed to fill the cabin that, like the rest of the ship's interior, did not accommodate his height. He was forever knocking his head against a lintel or crossbeam. It seemed that he kept his desires locked away inside him, rarely indulge in them, too concerned about duty. Antonia was glad that she could free him for a while.

'I can remember seeing you in a gown,' he muttered close to her ear. 'You were lovely.'

'But these days I wear breeches and carry a sword,' she answered, turning it into a joke lest her heart break. The prince rarely handed out compliments.

'No matter; I know what you're like beneath them.' He pulled at her shirt and she removed it, and the remainder of her clothing followed swiftly. So did his.

The bunk was narrow and hard and in no way long enough for him, but to her it was paradise. No grand seigniorial couch could have served her purpose better. His weight was heavy on her, until he propped himself up on his elbows and scrutinised her face, then her breasts. He kissed and nuzzled them, and she wondered how much mothering he had received from Elizabeth of Bohemia. Not a lot, from what he had just told her.

She responded, careful not to reject him in any way, lying beside him and relishing his splendid frame, honed by years of fighting and riding. As far as she was aware she was the only woman he'd had, since that time when he was drunk and she had angrily dismissed the whores. His close companion was his brother, Maurice. Yet just for an hour he was hers.

It was an hour of passion during which he indulged his lust, using the means she had taught him to insure that she, too, was fulfilled. His strength and power was what she needed in a man. She was borne along by it as if by a tempest, hurrying her own climax so that he could reach his, not once but several times.

When they lay replete at last she listened to the activity on deck and felt the gentle rise and fall of the vessel, and Rupert's hand in hers and his regular breathing as he slept, and she asked for nothing more.

When next she saw Mark she sounded him out concerning Judith. 'You haven't sent word to her?'

His face was stern as they stood together on the poop deck, the wind in their faces. The ship was sailing across the English Channel towards Calais. 'I have, but imagine that she never received them. You know how difficult it is to communicate by letter. Or perhaps she did, and has decided to cut me out of her life forever.'

'I doubt this. She promised to marry you, didn't she?'

'Yes, but that was a long time ago. Who knows what has happened to her, especially if she has been living with Isobel. You are aware of that lady's reputation. Judith may have had a dozen lovers by now.'

'Does this matter if she is yours in the end?'

'Perhaps not. Who knows? We may not like one another when we meet again after so long.'

'True. Time changes people, but wait and see what happens. You can rely on me.'

205

Life at Isobel's had become almost routine. For Judith it consisted of keeping herself presentable always, welcoming guests, for Isobel was hostess to several who did not visit her purely to indulge their fancies. She entertained writers and artists, musicians and nobility. Her house became a meeting place for philosophers, visionaries and those eager to improve the lot of the common man. Judith's concepts had expanded while listening to their discussions.

There were serious-minded women too, rebelling because they were not encouraged to paint or write anything other than sentimental poetry or insipid watercolours. As for education, or becoming a teacher or a doctor? This was out of the question and they were laughed to scorn by the male members of their families, but not in Isobel's house.

Henri was still Judith's friend and sometime bed companion, but one day he came to her and said, 'I'm to be married.'

This was something of a surprise, although she had guessed it would happen one day. 'When?' she asked, pausing by the folly, a miniature Greek temple that ornamented the garden.

'Early next year,' he said, leaning against a pillar and staring into the distance.'

'Who is she?' Although she wasn't in love with him, still hankering after Mark, the idea of losing him was hurtful.

'An heiress. It has been arranged between our parents ever since we were born, as happens among families of our class.' He looked resigned, but hastily added, 'It won't change my life too much. I shall leave her at my estate in the country and spend most of my time in Paris. Her duty will be to produce children.'

'Will she be happy about this arrangement?' Judith questioned.

'She'll have no choice. She seems to be an obedient little thing. I'll bring her to Court sometimes for a treat.'

'Dear God, you are beginning to sound like all the other men, and I thought you were different,' Judith commented, exasperated.

He tried to take her in his arms. 'Calm down, *cherie*. I will be kind to her, and I think she is already in love with me.'

Judith struggled free. 'Go away! Don't think you can come here and be unfaithful to her with me.'

'Will you accept an invitation to the wedding?' He was looking at her in that charming, roguish way of his, hard to resist.

Judith tossed her head. 'I might, if time allows. I am very busy, you know. Will you tell her about me?'

'It is none of her business. Besides, what is there to tell?'

He was unrepentant and she could do nothing but smile, forgive him and send him on his way. But his news underlined the loneliness of her existence. Oh, she was surrounded with people, helped keep the accounts, kept an eye on the staff, attended parties, took drives in the park and had seats at the theatre, but inside she felt bleak. There had been no news of Mark.

'What is wrong?' Isobel asked, coming into Judith's bedroom later that evening.

'Henri is to be married.' Judith was on a stool before her dressing-table, gloomily searching her face for signs of aging.

207

Isobel sat on the bed. 'So? You knew this would happen one day. I don't suppose it will change his mode of life much. Like most husbands he will be a law unto himself.'

Judith slammed down her hairbrush. 'Where is Mark?'

'On the high seas playing pirates, I imagine.' Isobel patted the space beside her. 'Come over here, sweetheart. Stop fretting. You are doing a fine job of helping me run this place. I don't know how I would manage without you. Mark will turn up like a bad penny one day.'

'Do you really think so? You're not just saying that?' Judith was comforted to feel Isobel's arms around her.

'I have a good feeling about it.' Isobel kissed her softly. 'Meanwhile, why don't we forget about men for a while? Let me share your bed tonight.'

It was too appealing an offer to refuse and Judith melted into her arms, longing for comfort as well as sensual enjoyment. She remembered her introduction to this form of loving when Antonia was a captive at Ferris Mead. It had turned her life around, and she had never regretted it. Now she enjoyed Isobel's attentions, sweet as a sister, caring as a mother and exciting as a lover. Their gowns were laced at the back, and they helped each other to undress, stretching and massaging their released ribcages with sighs of relief.

'It was so much easier when I wore shirts and breeches,' Judith commented.

'I must try it. My dressmaker says it is now fashionable for ladies to wear breeches beneath their riding skirts.' Isobel untied the drawstring around her petticoats and they slithered to the carpet. All that remained was her lace-trimmed chemise and, when this had been discarded, she lifted her arms over her head, her magnificent breasts rising.

Judith, also nude, could not resist reaching out to caress the dark nipples, and they hardened even more. 'Sweetheart, why do we bother with men when we have this?' Isobel smiled.

'It is good to enjoy both,' Judith said as they sat shoulder to shoulder. There was no need to hurry; they had hours in which to explore and enjoy each other's delightful female flesh.

Isobel ran a hand up the length of Judith's thigh, brushing against her fair bush and carrying on upwards, past her navel towards her breasts. Judith shuddered in anticipation, and was not disappointed. Isobel's touch was just right, rousing her, sending quivering shocks straight down to her groin. Together they lay back on the bed, the more to be able to fondle, give pleasure and receive it too.

The flames crackled in the ornate fireplace and candles glowed, throwing a soft light in which everything seemed magical, including their bodies. Soft mattress beneath them, clean linen sheets, a feather quilt such as was used in Europe and a coverlet woven in India; it was all conducive to stirring the senses.

Judith turned into Isobel's warmth and they started to caress and kiss, revelling in one another. Their passions were mounting and they were about to explore further when there came a sharp knock on the door.

Isobel sat up and reached for her robe. 'Who is it?' she cried.

Her maid answered. 'My lady. You have visitors. They demand to see you.'

209

'Oh, very well. Bid them enter.' Isobel signalled to Judith to get something on, and then the door opened to admit Antonia – followed by Mark.

Judith thought she was about to die. There he stood, dusty and dishevelled, tanned and weary, yet very real as she found out when he grabbed her up into his arms. She laughed and cried, and so did Isobel when she embraced Antonia. There was so much to say, so many questions to ask and be answered, but for those first moments all they could do was hang on to one another.

Isobel had food brought up and wine, and they sat by the fire, and the travellers talked as if they would never stop. It seemed they had landed at Calais and made straight for Paris.

'Rupert has gone to St Germaine to see the Royal Family,' Antonia explained, grabbing hold of Isobel's hand. 'We shall be here for a while.'

Judith felt she was moving in a dream. She couldn't stop looking at Mark and he returned her gaze adoringly. Nothing had changed between them and it was not long before Isobel said, 'Come, Antonia, let us go to my chamber and leave these lovebirds alone.'

Antonia, looking even more like a dashing filibuster, kissed Judith and followed Isobel out.

Judith felt almost shy. There was so much to say and a lot of catching up to do. Mark seemed almost a stranger, older and tougher, with experiences under his belt that she could only begin to imagine. He stood when she did and they looked at each other, holding hands.

'So you help Isobel to run this house?' he began, but asked no more questions. It was almost as if he did not want to know what part she played in it.

'She has given me a home. Why didn't you write to me?'

'I did, but the letters must have gone astray. I've thought of you constantly. It was the memory of you that helped me through the difficult times at sea, the bombardment of Roundhead shipping and the everlasting danger.'

'Oh Mark, I have never forgotten you and prayed for your safety.' Judith erased Henri from memory. He was as nothing compared with this joy.

'Shall we be wed? I may have to go fighting again, but at least you will be my wife.'

He was holding her tightly as if he would never let her go, and Judith sobbed, 'Of course we'll be married, as soon as possible.'

'But first I want to lie with you and convince myself this is not a dream.' He took off his cloak and sword, and she backed towards him when he sat down, seizing one of his legs between hers and hauling at his boot. The other came next. 'I stink,' he said ruefully. 'I've been in the saddle for hours, but had to come straight here to find you.'

'You can clean up if you want.' She indicated the basin and jug on the washstand. 'I'll help you.'

He cast off his shirt and she admired his body, toughened and sun-browned by his adventures. She sponged his back while he applied a flannel to his face, looking at his stubble ruefully. 'I don't suppose you have a razor? No? I shall have to find a barber in the morning.' He dropped his breeches and washed his genitals.

Judith tried to look away, but the sight was too fascinating. All she wanted was to have him in her bed and in her arms, proving to her he was no phantom born of her longing. And he had spoken of their marriage! She could hardly believe it.

He used a towel to dry himself, and then turned to her. 'Do you still love me? I shall understand if you don't and have found someone else.'

'Yes, I love you. Believe me when I say that I help Isobel on the practical side in return for her providing me with a roof and food and clothing. She is so kind.'

'I know. That is good. Whatever you do or have done I shan't blame you. When you are my wife I hope to be able to provide for you. I shall have to continue as a soldier, for that is my only skill, until such time as I can return to my home in England.'

She wound her arms about him, holding him close, naked as he was. She wore nothing but a fragile nightgown, his heat penetrating it. He lifted her as if she was no lighter than a feather and carried her to the bed where he laid her down. She could not stop looking at him, still unable to believe the reality of him being there with her.

'Oh Mark, Mark, this is what I've longed for all these months. I've missed you so much,' she murmured, until he stopped her with kisses.

Then there was no time for talking. He was like a starving man expressing his need in fierce possession of her. It was as if they had never been parted. What she had experienced with Henri was nothing compared to this. She felt like a virgin, untouched by any man before. Mark controlled himself long enough to give her pleasure. It was as if her body was sacred and he wanted to familiarise himself with it all over again.

She was so hot for him that it took little time to reach her climax. She cried out as he penetrated her hard while she ground her pubis against him, her inner muscles clenching around his cock. It was a blissful mating, and afterwards they lay and talked and made plans and Judith had never been so happy.

'So you have returned to me, my soldier,' Isobel said, looking across to where Antonia stood, admiring her handsome features and the easy way in which she wore men's clothing, second nature by now.

Her hair was longer, her skin sun-kissed, and Isobel thought her a perfect amalgam of both sexes. She had guessed long ago that Antonia was devoted to Rupert, and that this even went further, but she never mentioned it, enjoying what she could with her beautiful friend. Antonia smiled at her; different somehow, what she had endured recently taking its toll.

She shook her head. 'Not so much a soldier as a sailor these days.'

'It doesn't matter which. You're here now and I'm so relieved to see you. Sometimes I feared you might be dead. Tell me about piracy. Are women passengers on enemy ships raped?'

Antonia made an impatient gesture. 'No, they are not. Sorry to disappoint you but I want to put it behind me for a while. I've had enough, but suppose I will go with Rupert again when he leaves France.'

Isobel held out her arms. 'Come to me, darling. My brave soldier, sailor or whatever you are. Welcome back.'

It was like the old days in Oxford. Isobel knew it was Antonia, yet could pretend she embraced a swashbuckler enjoying a break from killing and pillaging. She would not have tolerated such a person in real life, but it added an extra thrill to their lovemaking. Knowing her part in the charade

213

Antonia threw her onto her face, knelt between her thighs and tied her hands behind her back, while Isobel wriggled and protested, but not too much.

'Enemy bitch! Roundhead doxy!' Antonia muttered, forcing a hand between her legs and finding her wet and ready. 'Oh, so you like a bit of rough, do you? Well, deary, I'm a sea-wolf and you're about to get it!'

She turned Isobel over, her eager breasts, belly and cleft craving caresses. Antonia made her wait, feeding her appetite by pinching her own nipples and rubbing her clitoris while Isobel watched. 'Do it to me, please,' her victim begged, trussed like a fowl and unable to reach her needy spots.

'Wait until I've finished,' Antonia commanded, and brought herself to a swift climax before releasing Isobel and becoming a caring lover.

Isobel clung to her and Antonia took her time, caressing every erogenous zone and gradually raising her higher and higher until she screamed and reached the peak. 'Oh, Antonia,' she gasped, wriggling against those knowing fingers. 'I suppose you and I will have to marry men one day, to produce heirs if we ever get our estates back, but just for now I am content.'

Antonia settled back against the pillows and her face was serious. 'I have no idea when this may be. The Parliament has won and they are out to capture King Charles. The future looks bleak for him and his followers.'

'But he is the king, appointed by God to rule England,' Isobel protested, although never bothering her head with politics. 'They can't take that away from him, can they?'

'I suppose not.' Antonia didn't sound too sure, but

Isobel, having rested, wanted to play games again, and they did, far into the night.

If the service in the church was a quiet affair, as befitted a widow, then the wedding reception was certainly not. Isobel revelled in celebrations and this was the marriage of her two friends, Judith and Mark. She and Antonia had been matrons of honour, using it as an excuse to have new gowns made for the occasion.

The mansion buzzed with excitement, for Judith had made a number of friends, and even Henri was there with his bride. 'Congratulations, *ma belle*,' he whispered to Judith. 'So he returned to you. I hope you will be very happy. But never forget that I am here, should you need me to keep you satisfied when he is absent.'

'Oh, Henri, you are incorrigible,' she replied, shocked but flattered.

'Meet my wife.' He drew the shy young lady forward. 'She is already with child. Will you be producing an infant?'

'I hope so,' she replied, smiling at the girl who, starry-eyed, was gazing at Henri.

Judith stood with Mark, receiving their guests. This was nothing like her sparse first wedding when her parents had not believed in merry-making, and neither had Steven. She wondered, not for the first time, if they were still alive.

Now she was the centre of attention and enjoying the warmth of her friends' affection. Mark had applied for a post as bodyguard to the French king, recommended by Rupert, and this would mean they could rent a house of their own in Paris and settle down as a couple. She thought she might miss the stimulation of Isobel's ménage, especially when he was on duty, but this would be another adventure and she had survived so many all ready. Just to have him close and safe was all she asked for the moment.

Now, everyone fortified with fine wine and good food, came the time when the bride and groom would be put to bed, as was the custom. First she was taken to her room and undressed by her matrons of honour.

'Don't you wish you were an unsullied virgin?' Isobel giggled, helping her out of the magnificent bridal gown, not white as she had been married before, but of ivory silk, suitable for wearing on other occasions.

'I'm not sure. I don't think so. I was terrified on my first wedding night.' Judith recalled it with a shudder. 'I knew nothing, and Steven was rough and uncaring. He made no attempt to please me.'

'Forget it,' Antonia advised, resplendent in the latest fashion, hardly recognisable out of men's garb. 'Mark is a fine fellow and truly loves you. I suppose this will happen to me one day, when we return to England and I can reclaim my property.'

'Me too,' Isobel chipped in, dropping the cream silk nightgown over Judith's head. 'I need to carry on my family name. When will this happen, do you think?'

Antonia shrugged. 'Who knows? I fear for King Charles should the Roundheads capture him. I can't see Oliver Cromwell relinquishing power.'

'Hush,' Isobel cautioned. 'No politics tonight. This is a time for rejoicing and pleasure, and when we have put the couple to bed we can do what we want to, follow our fancies and make it a time to remember.' She clapped her hands, and the other ladies who had come up to join in the ceremony

216

listened as she said, 'Come, let us bring in the bridegroom.'

He had been prepared by the gentlemen in an adjoining room, and was led in to a chorus of advice with regard to the carrying out of his husbandly duties. Amidst the banter and teasing he approached the marriage bed and Antonia whipped back the covers so that he and Judith could take up their positions within it. Everyone cheered and bid them goodnight before taking themselves off to continue the celebrations.

Mark slid an arm around Judith's shoulders. 'What a fuss,' he laughed. 'But they are all well-meaning. Are you happy, dearest?'

'Oh yes,' she sighed, nestling against him. 'I can't believe it is true.'

They had stayed apart for a week, and the first time he had seen her was at the altar. Now their hunger for each other blotted out anything else. His mouth possessed hers, their tongues entwining. She was so eager and pressed her breasts against his chest as he lay beside her, one long leg covering her thighs.

I'm really, truly married to him! she thought, while thought was at all possible, and she raised herself, pushing him back so that she might sit astride him and look down into his face. He was tense, his erect prick rising up between them. Judith fondled it, exposing the helm and at the same time palpating her clitoris. Mark reached for her breasts and his touch on her nipples accelerated her rise to climax.

He moved, lifting so he could penetrate her wet sex. 'Let me,' he said, substituting her finger for his on her aroused bud.

She braced herself on her arms, feeling him penetrating her deeply, controlling his thrusts until she was ready. Almost there she could feel her orgasm peaking. Mark slowed to prolong her ecstasy, but she was too far gone, plunging into a climax so fierce and exquisite that she lost grip on reality for a moment. Then he rounded off the experience by rolling her over, still impaled on his cock, and thrusting into her again and again until his semen burst from him, filling her.

Replete, Judith allowed herself to believe that her dream had come true. By leaving her Puritan background she had fought, suffered, known hardship, but it had led to this wonderful end. When the conflict was finally over, maybe they could return to their homeland and settle there, but yesterday was gone and tomorrow had not yet happened. She had the present with Mark and she was content.

Epilogue
England 1660

Judith stood in the Great Hall of Ferris Mead. Although fifteen years had passed since she was last there every memory was clear. She could almost see Steven and feel the lash as he humiliated her. The person who stood before her somewhat resembled him, his nephew, Nicolas Ashley.

He stepped forward, an upright man, soberly dressed but with an open smile. 'Welcome, Lady Granger,' he said. A plump woman stood just behind him with two lads. He introduced them. 'May I present my wife, Margaret, and these are my sons, Richard and Andrew.' She curtsied and they bowed.

Mark's hand was warmly encouraging under Judith's elbow, supporting her through this meeting that was bound to be difficult. Her old home could be hers again, if she wanted it. Though in exile for so long, particularly after Charles I had been tried as a traitor and then publicly beheaded outside his own palace at Whitehall, London, at the end of January 1649. Judith remembered the shock that had rippled through Europe. The execution of a king had not happened for hundreds of years, and it alarmed reigning monarchs.

Now the Royalists were coming home. Oliver Cromwell, who had set himself up as Lord Protector, had died and there was no one to take his place. In the end Charles II, after kicking his heels in France for so many years, had been invited to return, although the Divine Right of Kings would never give him the power of his ancestors. He had to work with Parliament.

The populace were delighted, tired of the strict rule of the Puritans. Judith had heard it said that when the thirty-year-old Charles rode through London on his return he was greeted so enthusiastically that he cynically remarked to a companion, 'If I'd known they wanted me back so much, I'd have come earlier.'

Judith had been presented to Charles, a darkly saturnine, handsome man, who loved women, the theatre, science, clocks and miniature spaniels, in that order.

They had all followed the king. Isobel had long before sold her business to Lola Diago, but still kept open house in her new abode. She'd married Jamie

Westbury, a biddable person who had done his duty and provided her with three children, a daughter, followed by two boys. Fond of one another they went their separate ways until the news had come through that they were free to return and claim their inheritances. Frankie, after years of soldiering, had taken over her father's farm in Ireland, and married a neighbouring squire. Tom and Emma and their six offspring had been retained by Isobel, faithful members of her staff.

Antonia's story was much the same, except that she had roamed the Caribbean with Rupert for several years, carrying out acts of piracy against the Parliamentarians. Then she returned to France while he went off fighting for whoever would employ him. Antonia, like a fish out of water, eventually met and married a younger man in order to produce heirs. With him she had come back to England and recovered her estate. Rupert had been given a position in which he was to build up the British navy.

So far Judith had not been able to meet up with either her or Isobel, but she hoped to do so once her affairs at Ferris Mead were settled. Leaving Paris had been a wrench, for she'd become accustomed to seeing her friends and their offspring, her own son and daughter playing with them. Sometimes Mark was away, guarding King Louis XIV when he went travelling, and then she stayed with Isobel, who still liked to entertain and whose house had become a centre of culture.

Thinking of this Judith talked to Nicholas. 'You have been running Ferris Mead for years and I have no wish to take it over. I shall settle at my husband's estate, so you are welcome to remain here.'

An expression of relief and delight lit his face. 'My

lady, that is most generous. What do you say, Margaret? We shan't have to uproot the children.'

'I'm very glad,' Margaret exclaimed. 'Thank you, Lady Granger.'

'I hope we shall remain friends,' Judith said, though having an inkling that they might still be too Puritan for her. England, especially London, was going wild now so many restrictions had been lifted, and she guessed that Isobel would be in her element, throwing open her townhouse and welcoming all to her parties.

'Won't you stay with us for the night?' Nicolas asked. 'You would be more than welcome.'

'No, thank you,' she said quickly, horrified at the thought of sleeping in the house that was redolent of Steven. 'I want to get back to the children. By the way, is Mrs Moffat still here?'

'Oh, no,' he said firmly. 'We found her to be dishonest and dismissed her. Mr Barnes went too, and we put members of our own staff in their place.'

There is justice in the world after all, Judith decided.

She and Mark entered their coach and began the journey to Wiltshire and their home. She already loved it, and had left the children there with their nursemaids. Being a mother was deeply satisfying, and her firstborn was a boy they'd called Simon, and then she had a girl, Rebecca, both born in Paris, so they could speak French like their own language. She was intensely proud of them, completely fulfilled, and there was the possibility of more to follow. She enjoyed motherhood. Soldiering had been an adventure and she did not regret a moment of it, but this was better.

She laid her head back against the upholstery,

wearing the latest thing in travelling attire, in dark-green velvet with the jacket cut like a man's and a full skirt. Mark was seated beside her and her heart flipped over at the sight of him, so reliable and good-looking.

'I'm glad that is over,' she said. 'They seem a genuine pair, and I don't want to have anything to do with a property once owned by Steven.'

They stopped off at taverns along the way, changing the horses and resting the coachman and armed grooms that had accompanied them. The roads were plagued by robbers, and vehicles were often attacked and needed to be guarded.

'You were one of them once, when you kidnapped me,' she said softly, and he kissed her and rested a hand on her knee.

'I did indeed, my love,' he said, lifting her skirt and caressing her inner thigh as he added, 'If we don't reach our destination soon I shall be forced to take you here and now.'

'Really, my lord!' She pretended to be outraged. 'What a suggestion to make to a young maiden.'

This seemed to make him even more determined, and he found her bud and fondled it in such a way that she reached a swift climax. It was as well, for the carriage stopped soon after and he helped her rearrange her clothing before they alighted and entered the Rose and Crown tavern. Before retiring they ate and drank, and made sure that the grooms were equally well-treated.

Judith had become used to staying in inns during the journeying she'd done lately. It reminded her of days in the army, and she and Mark were inclined to reminisce.

'Did it really happen?' she mused, as he climbed

into bed beside her. 'I can't imagine having the courage now.'

'They were stressful times and what good did it do? All those hundreds of lives lost.' Mark could be quite serious when the subject was raised. Now the Earl of Marshfield, inheriting from his father, he had taken over the role wholeheartedly and she was sure he would prove to be a just landowner, caring for those who were his responsibility.

'I want to see the children.'

'Dearest, you've only been away a few days,' he chuckled, cradling her in his arms. 'I'm glad to have you to myself for once.'

'Can we invite Antonia and Isobel to visit? Simon and Rebecca are missing their playmates.'

'Of course. You ladies can gossip while Jamie and I and Jean-Paul go hunting. I'm quite sorry for that young husband of Antonia's. French viscomte he may be, but he is right under the thumb.' Mark nuzzled into her neck, willing to agree to almost anything if she would only stop talking and concentrate on him.

'He loves to be dominated and she wants to rule the roost, so both are content.' Judith visualised long days when the men were chasing deer, the children were in the charge of their nursemaids and the three women were alone together, enjoying the pleasures of the senses. Happily married and mothers though they were, they still rejoiced in each other's bodies when the opportunity arose.

Mark was kissing her and caressing her willing flesh and she thanked whatever deity had shaped her life, freeing her from her former restrictions, opening the world for her and leading her to Mark, her partner, husband and lover.